T0054251

You Call That Service?

Too embarrassed to watch Ouka bite into his skin, Ryouta looked away.

Somehow, she looked even more vulnerable while sucking his blood than she did when she was sleeping.

The bus slowly crossed the border into the city of Oshiro.

"I wonder how Shiren's doing..."

©Hiroki Ozaki

CONTENTS

©Hiroki Ozaki

7

KISETSU MORITA

Illustration by

HIROKI OZAKI

YEN
ON
New York

You Call That Service?, Vol. 7

Kisetsu Morita

Translation by Jasmine Bernhardt
Cover art by Hiroki Ozaki

This book is a work of fiction. Names, characters, places, and incidents are the product of the author's imagination or are used fictitiously. Any resemblance to actual events, locales, or persons, living or dead, is coincidental.

OMAE NO GOHOSHI WA SONO TEIDOKA? volume 7
Copyright © 2013 Kisetsu Morita
Illustrations copyright © 2013 Hiroki Ozaki
All rights reserved.
Original Japanese edition published in 2013 by SB Creative Corp.

This English edition is published by arrangement with SB Creative Corp., Tokyo in care of Tuttle-Mori Agency, Inc., Tokyo.

English translation © 2023 by Yen Press, LLC

Yen On
150 West 30th Street, 19th Floor
New York, NY 10001

Visit us at yenpress.com
facebook.com/yenpress
twitter.com/yenpress
yenpress.tumblr.com
instagram.com/yenpress

First Yen On Edition: February 2023
Edited by Yen On Editorial: Emma McClain, Anna Powers
Designed by Yen Press Design: Liz Parlett

Yen On is an imprint of Yen Press, LLC.
The Yen On name and logo are trademarks of Yen Press, LLC.

The publisher is not responsible for websites (or their content) that are not owned by the publisher.

Library of Congress Cataloging-in-Publication Data
Names: Morita, Kisetsu, author. | Ozaki, Hiroki, illustrator. | Bernhardt, Jasmine, translator.
Title: You call that service? / Kisetsu Morita ; illustration by Hiroki Ozaki ;
    translation by Jasmine Bernhardt ; cover art by Hiroki Ozaki.
Other titles: Omae no gohoshi wa sono teidoka?. English
Description: First Yen On edition. | New York, NY : Yen On, 2019–
Identifiers: LCCN 2019036814 | ISBN 9781975305628 (v. 1 ; trade paperback) |
    ISBN 9781975305642 (v. 2 ; trade paperback) | ISBN 9781975316754 (v. 3 ; trade paperback) |
    ISBN 9781975325046 (v. 4 ; trade paperback) | ISBN 9781975325060 (v. 5 ; trade paperback) |
    ISBN 9781975325084 (v. 6 ; trade paperback) | ISBN 9781975325107 (v. 7 ; trade paperback)
Subjects: CYAC: Vampires—Fiction. | Love—Fiction. | Humorous stories.
Classification: LCC PZ7.1.M6725 Yo 2019 | DDC [Fic]—dc23
LC record available at https://lccn.loc.gov/2019036814

ISBNs: 978-1-9753-2510-7 (paperback)
        978-1-9753-2511-4 (ebook)

10 9 8 7 6 5 4 3 2 1

LSC-C

Printed in the United States of America

Characters

Ryouta Asagiri

A second-year high school student who wandered into the Sacred Blood Empire. He is cursed to be extremely attractive to human females. He became Shiren's minion and now lives with her.

Shiren Fuyukura

There was some distance between Shiren and her older sister, the emperor, because Shiren is the daughter of someone suspected of assassinating the previous emperor, but they recently made up. Ryouta's master.

Ouka Sarano

The current emperor, who claimed independence from Japan for the Sacred Blood Empire. Shiren's big sister. An old friend of Ryouta's from elementary school.

PROLOGUE

"C-can I eat *all* of this, Mom…?"

Dozens of large plates sat before Shiren.

She was presently standing before the buffet in a very fancy hotel.

"Of course. You can eat as much as you like, sweetie. We're renting the top floor of this hotel to live in, after all. We get to eat here every day as part of the agreement. Building a house like a palace would be very expensive, and it would attract too much attention, wouldn't it? And just thinking about the security gives me a headache. That's why I thought we should make our home in a hotel for the time being. And besides," Sairi added emphatically, "meals should be all-you-can-eat. That's just fundamental."

"I'm impressed, Mom. You really understand cuisine. Food *should* be free. It shouldn't be bound by the constraints of day-to-day life. We should eat what we want, however much we want—that is the true delight of mealtime."

"That's my girl! You know your—"

Shiren was loading her plate with food before Sairi had even finished speaking.

"Salisbury steak, scrambled eggs, gratin, simmered chicken… Oh, my plate's almost full. Time for a second one."

She began ferociously piling food onto her second plate, too.

It was not long before she'd filled her plates; each one looked like she'd ordered an extra-large helping at a restaurant with unusually generous portions.

"Three kinds of curry? That means I'll have to split my rice into three. Can I eat this much? There are three kinds of soup, too. I think I can handle that. They offer a choice of rice or bread? Well, I'll just have to eat both, then."

"Shiren, there is no rule stating you have to eat everything."

"Please—it'd be arrogant to simply pick one over the others. I could never do something so rude to the chef. *Munch*—I am going to—*munch*—eat everything, even if I explode."

It seemed mealtime came at a cost after all.

Shiren started with a bite of the Salisbury steak.

"Let's pretend there's someone here with—*munch*—seven children. Do you think they—*munch*—decide to simply not love one because they have so many? *Munch*—of course not. They would love all seven equally. It's exactly the same as a buffet."

"You've matured since I last saw you, Shiren."

Though all this made little sense, Sairi was still moved. There was the faintest hint of tears in her eyes.

"Then I shall join you," she said, "and eat some of everything."

Sairi began piling food on her plate, following Shiren's example. Her food was arranged much more neatly than Shiren's, but that meant she was using a lot more plates.

Sairi Fuyukura, as it happened, was just as much of a gourmand as her daughter.

Within minutes, this mother and daughter's plates had completely covered a table meant to seat eight.

"Well, should we make a toast to the Holy Sacred Blood Empire? (Even though you've already started eating.)"

"Yes, Mom."

Sairi lifted a glass of red wine, and Shiren a glass of tomato juice.

Clink.

A clear ringing sound echoed from their two glasses.

"Oh, this is good! Delicious! Every single ingredient shines through, and none have been wasted! The seasoning is not competing with the food. Really, this is an excellent display of food-seasoning teamwork. Yes—yes! Cooking is not about the chef beating the ingredients into submission.

No, a chef must meet the ingredients where they stand and guide them to greater heights. The chef here understands this!"

Shiren was shoving food into her mouth with astonishing speed.

At some point, a smear of ketchup had materialized at the corner of her mouth.

"It sure seems that way," Sairi replied. "I doubt there were any high-level chefs like this back in the old Empire."

"Is the 'old Empire' the Sacred Blood Empire in Akinomiya?" Shiren tilted her head at the unfamiliar phrase. She did not stop eating, however.

"Yes. We are the new Empire, and that is the old Empire, though it isn't as if the old Empire is gone. But for the time being, let us concentrate on our meal."

"You're exactly right. They could never serve food with such refined flavors in the old Empire. There were many times I wanted to shout, *Bring out the manager!* But not even the castle had a manager, all because the Empire was trying to cut costs."

"I don't think that part was about cutting costs. Castles just don't typically have managers..."

"There were top-rate chefs, but no one truly at the pinnacle of culinary ability. Such cuisine isn't just about flavors; it's about ideas."

The old Empire's greatest weakness was its closed-off nature and stagnation (particularly of its cash flow). And when it had a population of less than fifty thousand, even its top chefs were bound to be less than astounding.

The Holy Sacred Blood Empire, on the other hand, was more of an institution situated in Oshiro. There were essentially no hard borders, and the headquarters were located in Japan.

But that also put them in contact with the whole rest of the world.

"This is part of your education, Shiren."

"Education? Sorry, I break out in a rash when I hear words related to school..."

"I think that's a rather excessive reaction... Besides, this is not that kind of education."

"What do you mean, then?"

"You are the emperor of the Holy Sacred Blood Empire. We cannot allow our ruler to have cheap taste. You've only eaten commoner food thus far, haven't you?"

"Yes... My meals were always simple... After all, our finances were pretty tight..."

Though Shiren received money through a pension system, Ouka was stingy, and so the amount was pretty small.

"But even the cheapest snacks have their own unique charm. There is a kind of happiness that can only be attained from the taste of cheap—"

"I am fully aware, Shiren. I once took a trip specifically to eat a potato chip only available in one area of the country. I didn't even have a chair to sit down in, and I had to eat standing up." Sairi pouted. Clearly, she was not interested in hearing things she already knew.

This mother and daughter really got serious when it came to food.

"But," continued Sairi, "there are also flavors you cannot taste without paying lots of money. An emperor must become familiar with those, too."

"I see. I want to taste all the flavors of the world."

Shiren apparently found that statement much more impressive than it was, as she was full of pride.

"From now on, you must spoil yourself and find your dignity as emperor."

"Is this heaven?"

"No. This is the new Empire—the Holy Sacred Blood Empire." Once Sairi had finished swallowing her food, she continued, "I believe Ouka went through something very similar after becoming emperor."

"Come to think of it, I'm sure she had a personal chef..."

"One of my objectives is to provide you with an environment equal to that of the other emperor. On that point, I will accept no compromises."

"Why?"

Sairi gazed lovingly at Shiren, ketchup smear and all.

"Both you and Ouka have royal blood. But because I'm your mother, you've been given the short end of the stick all your life. One sister should not receive better treatment than the other simply because of the circumstances of their births."

"Oh…" Shiren had finally begun to understand Sairi's kindness.

"That is why I will give you everything Ouka has. I created the Holy Sacred Blood Empire so that *you* could be emperor, too."

"But I'm nowhere near as capable as Big Sis… I couldn't…"

Shiren's new status still hadn't sunk in, and she was well aware of her sister's abilities and all her hard work.

Ouka had gone through many trials in order to fulfill the role of emperor. Even after her father died, she never once complained as she rebuilt the organization that would eventually become a nation. It was her right to wield power as emperor.

Shiren had never once thought Ouka was treated favorably because of her birth, and though Shiren sometimes complained about her misfortunes, she had never once been upset that she wasn't emperor herself.

"You can do this, Shiren." Sairi smiled at her daughter. "I'll support you as archbishop. I won't ask you to run the whole institution at your age."

"My average test score is five percent."

"That's…that's pretty bad." Sairi was now fully aware of her daughter's lack of intelligence. "All right… I'll find you a top-class tutor."

"Is there anything I can just put on while I sleep that will make my scores skyrocket?"

"No cheating. You *will* study."

Shiren's scheme to take it easy had been immediately foiled.

"But we can still manage. This new empire will bring happiness to all the Sacred Blooded around the world. I'm sure of it." Sairi gave an easy smile.

Sairi, for her part, must have planned everything with the utmost care.

"All right. I'll do it!"

Shiren knocked back the tomato juice in her cup in one go, as though steeling her resolve. Drops of tomato juice joined the ketchup on her lips.

From now on, she was going to do what she needed to under Sairi's guidance. She had been ready for this the moment she chose to come to Japan with her mother. All she needed to think about now was acting as the emperor of the Holy Sacred Blood Empire.

She might not be full of confidence, but she didn't think it was impossible, either. She had Sairi with her, after all. She could do this. She knew she could.

Still, she felt like something was missing.

She had all the food from the buffet laid out before her, and she would soon start her new, luxurious life living out of a fancy hotel room, but... there was something lacking.

I'm not going to think about it. Shiren pushed away those thoughts.

She had a feeling the more she dwelled on it, the worse the feeling would get.

The news was a constant stream of reports on the Holy Sacred Blood Empire.

Ryouta could absorb only a few facts in his morning grogginess.

It called itself an empire, but it was not independent.

Essentially, it was an organization created by those who felt alienated by the Sacred Blood Empire in Akinomiya.

Shiren was the emperor, and Sairi was the archbishop.

It was regrettable that the new Empire was calling our country the old Empire, but since it makes the two easier to distinguish, we'll be using these terms, too-. (On this point, Ryouta was reminded how lax this country always was.)

That was all. The rest was too complicated to understand from breaking news reports.

"This is crazy...," Ryouta commented in a daze.

He had just woken up and was sitting on his hospital bed when he heard the news. The shock was so great that his mind had yet to catch up.

"Indeed. This is quite the situation."

"Yeah. I had no idea something like *this* would happen while I was sleeping. I was hoping it was some kind of April Fools' joke, but it's the wrong time of year."

"Lady Ouka will certainly become very busy, and I plan to mass-produce stuffed dolls in her likeness to soothe her. They will all be handmade, but if I up my pace, I should be able to make three in a day."

"I think that's three too many to be making in a day— Huh?"

Sasara was standing by Ryouta's bed.

She was covered in wounds, supporting herself with a crutch.

"I'd not imagined I would wake up first. I was more gravely injured than you were."

"Are you okay, Sasara?"

"I would not need a crutch if I were okay. I am…supposed to rest for a while…"

"I'm sorry… I didn't turn out to be any help at all…"

Ryouta had been completely out of his element in the fight between Sairi and Sasara. In fact, he'd probably made things worse by distracting Sasara.

"I will pummel you if you continue to give meaningless apologies." Sasara glared at him. "We both did our best. So what if we ended up losing? Or do you mean to say you were going easy on her?"

"Of course not!"

"Then isn't that good enough?" Sasara smiled. Her expression was so calm, it was hard to believe she was injured.

"Thanks, Sasara…"

"There is no need for you to thank me in this situation. I will be returning to my bed."

There was an open bed across the passageway from Ryouta's.

"Wait, are you sleeping over there…?"

"We were both emergency cases, so we got crammed in together. I was worried you might not wake up, but you seem to be conscious now."

"You've been thinking about me this whole time…? Thank you…"

"I—I told you, I have done nothing to earn your thanks!" Sasara's face immediately flushed. She whispered, "After all, I doubt there will be any more time for me in the spotlight…" She sounded lonely. "Well, I'll be returning to my bed… It is quite painful to keep standing… Ah—"

Sasara lurched to the side. It seemed she'd lost her balance. She toppled over and landed right on top of Ryouta, followed by the sound of her crutch clattering to the floor.

"Hey! Are you okay?!"

"I am, yes, but…I cannot stand without my crutch…"

"So you can't move…"

Inevitably, Ryouta had caught Sasara in a kind of embrace, and their bodies were now pressed up against each other. Sasara's face was buried in Ryouta's chest.

"It seems you don't have much strength, either, Ryouta Fuyukura."

"I hate to admit it, but I *did* just wake up..."

Ryouta was in no state to even help Sasara back up at the moment.

"I should press the button to call a nurse... I think it was on the wall..."

He pressed the button.

"We will be making a stop shortly. Thank you for riding with us today."

"Why is this a bus button?! I wasn't looking before, but this is obviously a bus button!"

"It seems to be a construction error. They are rather similar, so perhaps the builder mixed them up."

"How do you mix those up?! No one mixes those up; they don't look alike at all! Nurse-call buttons are big so that sick or injured people can easily press them! Bus buttons are small so you don't hit them accidentally!"

"I have no need for such detailed criticism, thank you."

"I guess living in this country has made me more nitpicky... That said, even this bus button should be connected to the nurse's office if they've got it installed in the hospital, right?"

"Hello, how can I help you?"

A staticky voice could be heard from the interphone on the button.

"See? It *was* the nurse-call button. Uh, hello! I'm a patient here in room... Uhh... What's our room number...?"

The number 13 hung over the entrance.

"...Could you please come to room 13? Sheesh, what an unlucky number to put in a hospital."

"What? I'm sorry, but this is the office overseeing bus operations."

"Did they seriously hook this up to the bus system?!"

This was a pretty huge construction error.

"I suppose we have no choice but to wait in this position...," Sasara

©Hiroki Ozaki

murmured, still lying on top of Ryouta. "A nurse will surely pass by sooner or later. Look, there's a timetable on the wall."

"On the wall? Huh, so they have a schedule posted. I guess the hospital has it together in this department, at least."

Estimated Nurse-Arrival Times
9:36
11:20
14:07*
17:24
20:03*
(*Canceled on weekends or holidays) (Arrivals may be delayed depending on hallway congestion and treatment of other patients.)

"Don't make it like a bus schedule!"

While it seemed like a valid number of times for a nurse to drop by in the day, formatting it like a bus timetable made the stops sound way too far apart.

"I don't mind," said Ryouta, "but...are you sure you're okay waiting that long...? This seems a little inappropriate for a noble..."

"I-it is what it is... And this is far more manageable than being injured again. I could stay like this for hours; I could handle it every day..."

Even Ryouta could tell Sasara was nervous. He could see everything when they were this close.

"There's no way this would happen every day..."

"Well, this is only hypothetical, but if I was m-married, then I think things like this may happen often..."

"*Married...?*"

"I would not mind marrying you."

"Sorry, what.........?"

Depending on interpretation, that could be taken as a love confession.

"You have a lot of flaws, but they're all things I could make up for, if I worked hard… So I think it would turn out surprisingly well. And I believe we are rather compatible…"

"Um, Sasara? What do you mean by—?"

"This is all a what-if scenario, though." A sad smile crossed Sasara's face. "Congratulations on becoming Lady Ouka's minion."

That was when it all came back to him.

Ouka told me she'd always wanted to make me her minion…

"I don't appreciate the context of your well-wishing," came a sudden voice.

A shadow settled over Ryouta's face as a very irritated Ouka loomed before him.

"Whoa! Don't just show up like that!"

"Eeeeek! Lady Ouka, I just happened to fall, that is all…"

"I didn't think there would be any issues putting you in the same room since you were both injured, but look at you! Problems already! Give me a break! All right, Ryouta! You don't have any broken bones, so now that you're awake, you're released! Come with me! Go rest over there, Sasara!"

With Ouka's help, Sasara returned to her bed.

In the meantime, Ryouta got up, too, and found his footing to be surprisingly steady.

"Um, Lady Ouka…?" said Sasara. "All I was doing was giving you two my blessing…"

"Okay, I'll believe you. You seemed like you were backing off anyway."

"I appreciate it…"

"And please continue to take your surroundings into consideration when you act. It's your own fault if you don't seize a chance when you have it. You know that, don't you?"

"Yes… Everything is my fault… *Sigh.*" Sasara exhaled weakly, as if she was trying to exorcise her spirit, too.

Ouka patted her on the head.

"I'm glad you're a good listener. I'm counting on you to return to your position as my personal guard as soon as you're better."

"Of course! Thank you, Lady Ouka!"

"I know you'll find someone nice soon. No need to worry. Come to think of it, that cousin of yours—Toraha? He—"

"I have decided I shall continue to live for you and you alone, Lady Ouka."

"I have no idea what that is supposed to mean."

"You are the only one for me, Lady Ouka. I would like to return to my roots and rethink everything."

"I am not your roots!"

Sasara pulled something out from her bed—an Ouka body pillow.

"See? I am ready."

"For what?!" Ouka cried. "And when did you bring that in?!"

"It was part of a care package from my mother and father. They brought everything from my room."

"Your parents should've known to leave that at home!"

"Both of them were crying."

"Doesn't that mean they don't approve?!" Ouka got the feeling this conversation would never end and decided to cut it short. "We're going, Ryouta! We are getting as far away from that pillow as possible!"

"Yeah, good idea..."

Before he left the room, Ryouta's and Sasara's eyes met. For a moment, he hesitated, not sure what to say. It wasn't like they'd never see each other again, so why?

It was Sasara who spoke up first.

"I hope you find happiness."

"Yeah, thanks..."

"I will be sure to find my own." She smiled.

"Me too!" Ryouta replied, smiling back.

Ryouta was taken to the castle by car, then led inside to an area full of private rooms. It was exactly like the hallway in an apartment building. These must be the rooms provided to the castle staff.

"Now that you are the emperor's minion, you will receive a room as luxurious as your status."

"Huh, so this is really the start of a new life for me…"

It would be painful to return to the house he and Shiren had lived in together, so this was nice in a way.

There was a bright-red carpet spread across the floor, giving the surroundings an opulent feel.

"Here you go—room 1313 is all yours, Ryouta."

"First the hospital, and now my room? Am I cursed…?"

"The rooms next to you are 106 and 108, so I doubt you'll ever get lost."

"Then this should be room 107! Why am I the only one with a four-digit number?!"

"That's just how special your room is, as my minion. You should be honored."

"If you say so…"

"We performed a special exorcism just for the occasion. We even changed the number, so no one with a grudge tied to room 107 will show up."

"So something *did* happen here! You're putting me in a cursed room!"

"You'll be fine. Come on, let me show you around your new home."

She unlocked the door and opened it into a very large entryway. At this size, it was more than just an entryway—it was closer to the lobby of a building.

"Are these walls made of marble…?"

"The entryway is very secure. If anyone tries to get in without your permission, sensors will pick up on it and shock them."

"That sounds a little violent…"

"It's fine. You've been registered as a resident here, so it'll only react to people who force the lock open or try to get in through the window— Oh, there's someone on the floor…"

A singed Rei lay below them, collapsed. She had apparently tried to sneak in and failed.

"Even a ninja couldn't get past the security. It's working perfectly."

"Rei! Wake up! Rei! Oh no… Her heart's stopped… Her body feels cold. She's really dead…"

"Oh, she'll come back. Come on, chin up, let's keep going."

"My sister is dead! Aren't you being a little nonchalant?"

"She'd be of no use to me as a ninja if I got worked up over something like this!"

"I guess it's normal for her to lose consciousness when she has a fit…"

"Even after she fell into an industrial mixer and was ripped to shreds, she still came back to life."

"Are we sure she's actually a living thing?!"

"She made a mistake and fell into a bottomless swamp, but she still came back three days later."

"She's clearly not human!"

Just then, Rei did, in fact, wake up.

"I went to that flower field again. The man who told me he loved me last time was with another woman already… I hadn't planned on going out with him, but I'm still shocked…"

"You're back, so it's fine…," said Ryouta.

"Oh, and he asked me to do a job for him. He wanted me to deliver a message."

"Wow, Rei, you don't get scared at all. It must be because of all your near-death experiences!"

"Well, anyway. I'll pass on to my next job, then."

"I feel like there's something wrong with how you just worded that…"

"Well, I'll take my leave for now! I'll definitely manage to sneak my way in next time!"

"Please don't!"

Rei strode toward the door. Ryouta wondered if the sensor would activate when someone exited the room, and sure enough, a shock coursed through his sister.

"Aaaaaaah!"

"Rei! You really need to start learning your lesson!"

She recovered ten minutes later and finally left.

Even the sensor wasn't able to completely stop an immortal.

"It seems the sensor's crime-prevention mechanisms need work. We will have to upgrade the shock so it is capable of killing immortals."

©Hiroki Ozaki

"The power creep here is starting to confuse me…"

"Anyway, let me get back to showing you around your room… There's where you can store your shoes, and that's the hallway light switch, and there's a talisman on the wall behind the oil painting, but don't worry about it. That's where you'll put your washing machine when you get one—"

"Hold on! You can't just sneak in creepy info like that!"

"It's not creepy. The light switch is supposed to be big and easy to flip, in case an elderly person needs to use it. The shoe closet is big enough for lots of shoes, and you'll be provided a washing machine by the Empire."

"You skipped the part about the painting!"

"That painting is a masterwork. I got it for thirty-five hundred yen on Yahoo! Auctions."

"I'm not sure how much paintings are supposed to go for, but that sounds really cheap!"

"A painting's value is not in its price. Some leap straight to asking how much a great master's paintings cost, but that makes one look like a fool. I would advise against it."

"Actually, that's enough about the painting. Why is there a talisman behind it?!"

"Because some things just are."

"I'm not asking for a proverb here!"

"They're very popular with kids these days."

"That's definitely a lie!"

"This entire apartment unit is what we'd call a power spot. The talisman is there to regulate its energy. That's all."

"I'd prefer a room without any energy."

"As you live in this apartment, you'll gradually be blessed with more and more power from the spirits."

"So there *are* ghosts in here! That's gonna be an issue!"

In the end, they moved on without Ouka ever explaining the talisman.

"Here's the kitchen. You have storage space above you, and there's another talisman there, but don't worry about it."

"I will absolutely worry about it! What on Earth is written on it…?"

Ryouta peeled it from the wall to check.

*   *   *

COCKROACHES BE GONE

"See? I told you not to worry about it."

"Does this really work on cockroaches, though…?"

"Cockroaches that understand human writing are quite considerate, and if they see the talisman, they will leave right away."

"So it doesn't work at all, then."

"Also, there's a frying pan provided for you. It's even been treated."

"Oh, you mean it's been coated with Teflon?"

"No, I mean it's been warded against evil spirits."

"Please, can I just have a different room?! Why are you forcing this one on me?!"

"If an evil spirit attacks, all you have to do is hit it with the frying pan."

"You know, if things are that bad, you should just seal the room up…"

Once Ouka was finished showing Ryouta the kitchen, they moved on to the next room.

"Here's the bath. I think it's about five square meters."

"That's huge… The water, light, and heating costs for this bath alone must be crazy high…"

"Then why not use the public bath in the basement? There is a hot spring under the castle, you know. The public would be disgusted if they found out, so we try to keep it quiet."

"People in the castle sure are spoiled…"

"I wanted a private outdoor bath for the room, too, but that wasn't possible."

"Yeah. It's not like you could turn this whole place into an atrium."

Ryouta looked up at the ceiling; there were talismans plastered all over it.

"I think I'll use the public bath as much as possible…," he said.

"I appreciate your help saving water."

If Ryouta ignored the disconcerting talismans everywhere, the room felt very fancy.

"The balcony is over there. It has a great view."

"Huh. Let me take a look."

It certainly had a view—of the graveyard.

"All I can see are headstones!"

"Land near cemeteries is cheap, you see. It was a lucky find when I was looking into building the castle."

"I think we're starting to see the negative consequences of your focus on savings."

"See how the stones glint under the sun? Aren't you spellbound?"

"Who would be spellbound by graves?!"

"We've performed exorcisms, so you don't need to worry about them."

"You wouldn't need exorcisms if you hadn't built the castle next to a cemetery!"

"And in the morning, you might awaken to the singing of birds and the groans of the dead."

"I think I'll lock the windows when I go to sleep…"

The unit was certainly luxurious, but haunted vibes of each room mostly canceled it out.

"I have two more rooms to show you." Ouka came to stand before a closed door. "Though, I can't let you into this one yet. Sorry."

"It's haunted, right? I see where this is going."

Ryouta was pretty sure this must be the forbidden room where the ghost was sealed.

"That's where your handpicked selection of adult comics is stored. You can't go in there until you turn eighteen."

"Stop making pointless rooms like that!"

"You can use the erotica while you enjoy the view. It's quite romantic."

"You don't need to introduce romance into it, okay? And can you not use the verb *use*? At least say *read*!"

"Oh, it's not like you read every word on the pages filled with sound effects, do you? Some things you can skip over."

"Why are you even thinking about that?! And when you said *enjoy the view*—"

"I meant the graveyard."

"How can I enjoy *anything* with that graveyard out there?! I'm going to keep that room locked up forever! Just—just take me to the last room already, okay?"

"All right. The last room is the bedroom. This way."

The room was fresh and neat, and there were no talismans anywhere. It was the definition of luxury. The chic design utilized a black-and-white color scheme, and in the center sat a king-size double bed.

"Isn't this a little big for one person?"

"I'll be living here, too, so things have to be this big."

"Right. I guess that makes sen———————— What?"

Ryouta got the feeling he'd just heard something very shocking…

"But, Ouka, don't you have your own quarters…?"

Ryouta had seen her room with his own two eyes. It had been unexpectedly girly and cute.

"You see, my personal guards need to stay by my side at all times to protect me from assassins and Sasara. That is why they tend to be female."

"In that case, I suppose they do need to stay on high alert. I'll ignore the fact that you listed one of your own guards along with assassins as an equal threat."

"Now, consider the inverse. If I sleep in one of my guards' rooms to begin with, I'll be safe from danger. It won't be every day, of course."

"I kind of get where you're going with this now, but…you realize you'd be staying in a guy's room, right…?"

"Oh? Does that mean you're going to try something funny on Her Imperial Majesty?" Ouka stared hard at Ryouta, her gaze piercing.

"O-of course not…"

"Then there's no problem."

Ouka smiled, undaunted. She had calculated everything. Ryouta had no intention of arguing with her, nor was he in any position to do so.

"Okay… I promised I'd be your minion, so I'll protect you…"

"Exactly. You are my minion. I'm glad you remembered. So"—Ouka placed both hands on Ryouta's shoulders—"b-become my minion, officially."

Her expression suddenly turned apprehensive, like a switch had flipped inside her. It was almost as though the forceful personality from a few moments earlier belonged to a completely different person. Her voice had grown much quieter, too.

"Officially...?"

There was nothing wrong with the word itself, but something about the potential implications felt impure to Ryouta.

"Let me suck your blood, Ryouta. Become...mine."

A strange feeling overcame him, as though the blood were draining from his entire body.

"That means biting my arm or something, right...?"

"Yes. No one will see us here, so... D-don't make me say it out loud... I'm too embarrassed..."

Ouka's hands were shaking ever so slightly, and Ryouta could feel it radiate from his shoulders throughout his entire body. His heart thudded in time with her shuddering hands.

"C-can't we do this tomorrow...?"

"No... Once we put it off, it will be difficult to bring up again... You should know that..."

Ryouta got the feeling he genuinely *knew* how Ouka felt. His own feelings were scarily in tune with hers. He almost wasn't sure who the hands on his shoulders belonged to.

The only thing setting them apart was social standings.

"But Shiren— Oh, I guess that doesn't matter anymore."

Shiren Fuyukura was no longer in the Empire, nor was she Ryouta's master. Both Ryouta and Ouka had been present when that became a thing of the past. Ryouta's current master was right in front of him. His only master—one he would not confuse with another.

"Yes... Master..."

The moment those words escaped his lips, a strange feeling overcame him—something like freedom, along with a clenching in his heart. With this, the strange, hazy uncertainty that had hung over him would come to an end.

"All right. Ryouta, please sit on the bed..."

He did as he was told, and Ouka sat down beside him on his left.

"Hold out your arm. It might hurt, b-but tell me if it does, okay…?"

"Will you stop if I do?"

"No."

"Then there's no point. Well, a lot of people have bitten me so far, so I'm kind of used to it."

"Well, aren't you a hussy? It's not something people normally get used to."

"Yeah, you're probably right… I'll be more careful going forward…"

"You'd better. You're the emperor's minion now."

"I promise I won't be an embarrassment to you."

"And I will hold you to that—never forget that promise. Mental attitude is very important. There are two ways to earn respect: One is to accomplish something great in a particular field that everyone must then acknowledge; the other is to be a good person, to live so virtuously that one has no enemies at all. You have no incredible talents, Ryouta, so the least you can do is continue being a good person."

"So…are you going to bite me or not?"

Ouka's face flushed a bright, fiery red. Ryouta felt guilty, like he'd said something very mean.

"I-I'm embarrassed, okay? I thought I could hide it if I kept talking, but now it's making it even more difficult for me to commit… Just—just wait for me, okay?! This is my first time…"

"Wait, really? Don't you bite your guards?"

"L-look… Biting my female guards is different from biting a g-guy like you, Ryouta… You might not be Sacred Blooded, but… This is so weird. I've always wanted to do this, but now that my chance is right in front of me, I'm scared… *Weird* really is the only way to describe it. Please just understand…"

"Sorry… I should have been more tactful…"

"Okay, I'm doing it! I'm going in!"

She took Ryouta's arm.

"Oh," Ryouta suddenly piped up.

"Wh-what?"

"Should I go wash my arm off in the sink, or…?"

"No... You don't need to be that considerate..."

Ouka's eyes slipped shut, and she slowly sank her teeth into his skin.

Ryouta got through the first wave of pain by gritting his teeth.

The beginning was always the most painful, because the pain came from nowhere. After that, once a starting point for the pain had been established, it only throbbed a little in the same area.

Too embarrassed to watch Ouka bite into his skin, Ryouta looked away.

Somehow, she appeared even more vulnerable while sucking his blood than she did when she was sleeping.

I wonder if, seven years ago, I ever imagined I'd wind up here... There's no way.

Seven years ago, when Ryouta was living in Japan, every woman and girl had been his enemy. Every one of them had their sights on him on account of his curse. If it had just meant a lot of staring, it would have been fine, but on several occasions, he'd almost been kidnapped.

He got the feeling those girls didn't see him as a person, and to him, they weren't rational humans, either. It felt like he was the only person living in a forest full of monsters.

And then there was Ouka Sarano—the only girl who treated him like a person. The reason for that was simple. Ouka was Sacred Blooded, and she could retain her cool around Ryouta. The Sacred Blooded were totally unaffected by the curse.

Ouka was the only girl in his class who could look at him through unclouded eyes. In a way, it was only natural for Ryouta to start thinking of her as someone special. He adored her, and those feelings quickly turned into romantic affection.

Ouka wasn't like the other girls. She was the only one who treated me like a person. I was only human when I was with her.

That was why she had been his first crush and why, even after she transferred schools, his affection had remained frozen in time, never changing. There had been no one to replace her. Ouka alone was special to him.

I was only in fourth grade, and all I ever wanted to do was kiss her. I never thought about her biting me or anything like that. But you know, maybe this is good in its own way.

Ouka had been drinking his blood the whole while and couldn't speak. Unable to hold a conversation, Ryouta spent his time thinking about the past.

After seven years, his memories had only grown rosier and more beautiful. They could never be sullied.

Was this always my destiny…?

Maybe things had all fallen into place and led him here, to Ouka sucking his blood. Perhaps the pain in his arm had always been meant to be.

But the pain did not last for very long. It slowly vanished, and in its place came drowsiness.

This was a type of anesthesia. When a Sacred Blooded claimed a minion, they injected them with this substance to ease the pain. It was starting to take effect.

I can't sit up anymore…

Ryouta toppled backward on the bed. He had no strength left.

"Just a little while longer."

When he lay back, Ouka stopped for a brief moment to reassure him. Her tone was lazy; it was almost as though the anesthesia was working on her, too.

A string of her spit stuck to Ryouta's arm before breaking off. Ryouta could see she was sweating quite heavily. She was flushed, almost feverish.

Ouka lay down with him.

"I'm not done yet."

Once she started, she couldn't stop.

She grabbed Ryouta's arm and laid it across herself, then took it into her mouth. Nestling into him, she bit down.

"Yeah, keep going."

It didn't hurt anymore, so Ryouta wasn't entirely sure what was happening to him. His mind felt blank. He didn't have the energy to think about the past now, but strangely, he didn't feel like closing his eyes, either.

He was suddenly overcome with the impulse to hug Ouka, then absently scolded himself—they were master and servant, and that wasn't appropriate. He had a feeling the impulse had come to him because he wasn't in his right mind. He doubted Ouka would criticize him for it, but that was precisely why he thought he should wait for another day to hug her.

"I feel hot all over," he said.

He thought he saw her nod slightly. And then the strange three minutes—which at once felt extremely long and extremely short—came to an end.

"I think that should do it." Ouka slowly lifted her head.

"We're done? I feel weird—dazed. I don't think anyone's ever bitten me for three minutes before."

"You'd be in huge trouble if you let multiple people bite you for three minutes. Oh, Ryouta, you're still bleeding. We need to disinfect it—"

She pulled out a small packet of disinfecting wipes from her pocket.

"I guess that means everything's gone according to plan if you were carrying that around with you."

"Is that a problem?"

"No, not at all."

"Then yes, everything has gone exactly as I wanted." She smiled as she wiped his wound with gauze.

In contrast to her expression, her movements were clunky and awkward.

"Let me give you a simple command. We have to see if you've actually become my minion."

"Okay. If it worked, I should be able to sense something."

Ouka closed her eyes and made her wish.

After a little while, her thoughts came into Ryouta's mind.

Come closer to me. Come closer to me.

"I got them! I could feel what you wanted!"

"Really?!"

Ouka's eyes snapped open, and their gazes met. Then they looked away at the same time. She had just been drinking his blood, yet both of them felt awkward when it came to things like this.

"But why would you order me to do that...? I'm already really close to you..."

"It was just a test, okay...? It wasn't serious." She cleared her throat. "And be aware, I'm going to be picking on you a lot as my minion, so you'd best be ready for whatever I throw your way."

"Just be gentle, okay?"

"And with my stupid little sister gone, you'll have to take her share of bullying, too."

At that, Ryouta's expression clouded over.

"You…really are sad that she's gone, aren't you?"

"…Of course I am. Why wouldn't I be? But I was blessed with something else in return," she said, looking away from him. "I wouldn't have gotten you if she were still here."

The fact that she couldn't say that while looking at him only proved how large a hole Shiren's absence had left.

"Sometimes, we have to lose one thing to gain another. We were always going to have to take this step. It's like one's first day at a new school."

"You don't have to pretend like it doesn't bother you, Ouka."

"And you can say that you're mad at Shiren, Ryouta."

"Why would I be mad at her?"

"Don't you get it?" She turned to him again, sadness on her face. "She abandoned you."

Ryouta had nothing to say to that. He wanted to say she was wrong, but maybe she wasn't. Maybe that, too, was a part of the truth.

"You worked *so hard* for her. No one else in the entire world thought about her more than you did."

"But what else was I supposed to do? I can't replace her mother."

"I would never abandon you," Ouka said, her expression solemn and dignified. She was the picture of an emperor.

"I understand, Master."

"And your blood tasted *so* good, Ryouta. Better than any I've had so far."

"O-oh… I'm not sure if I should say thank you to that…"

"It was so good, in fact, that I almost want some more right now. But you'd faint if I did that, so I'll behave."

"There's nothing special about my blood," Ryouta said, embarrassed.

"But there is. To me, at least."

Meanwhile, Shiren was swamped with work at the Imperial office.

Though it was called the Imperial office, it was just one room in a building. This building was a Sacred Blooded holding some distance from the old Empire in Akinomiya. Apparently, it was being rented out by Sairi.

"Uhh... What does *stipulation* mean? Or *intercession*? And I'm sure this *conclusion* doesn't mean what I think it means. *Compensation of deficit*... I only know *compensation*. I think. *Implementation*? I feel like I should know what that means... Well, I kind of know a lot of these words, so I bet it's okay. I wish they'd use less fancy vocabulary! But it's probably fine. Imperial stamp time! Okay, next!"

Shiren was putting the Imperial stamp on every document.

"Keep at it, Shiren. You'll be doing that kind of work for a while yet."

Sairi was sitting opposite her, checking documents in much the same way.

"Don't worry, Mom. I'll just stamp everything and not worry about reading it."

"I would prefer it if you gave everything a once-over at least, but...that can be our next challenge to tackle. Keep on stamping!"

"Leave it to me! I'll break the stamping world record!"

"Oh, that's right. You'll need to make a speech to the new Empire's affiliates tonight. You need to think about what you want to say, Shiren."

"What? I don't have any time to think about that..."

"It doesn't have to be very long or complicated. You'll have to do a lot more things like this in the future."

The event that night was held at a hotel, a different one from where Shiren was staying. There were even Japanese politicians in attendance, ones she had seen on TV before.

First, New Progenitor Alfoncina—Sairi Fuyukura—came to the stage to speak.

"A surprising amount of time has passed since the Sacred Blood Empire was established in Akinomiya. It almost feels as though it has been there for decades now. I believe many of you here feel both pride that the Sacred Blooded were at last able to create their own country and, at the same time, apprehension that they have done so in such a messy, haphazard manner. As one who can trace her ancestry to the founder of the Holy Church of the

Sacred Blood, I had mixed feelings about the affair. I honestly questioned their sanity when I saw they were selling a swimsuit photo collection full of pictures of the archbishop."

She was, of course, talking about Alfoncina XIII, Matsuko Kimura.

Several of the attendees hung their heads. They must have purchased the photo collection.

"This sentiment continued to grow. We were frustrated beyond words that others might think *that* country represented all the Sacred Blooded. I racked my brain. What could I do? That was when I decided to create the new Empire—the Holy Sacred Blood Empire. Unlike the old Empire in Akinomiya, we aim to create a country that is conscious of the connection we have to the outside world. At the very least, we aim to think of our future as Sacred Blooded on Japanese soil. We already have plenty of non–Sacred Blooded helping and working with us. This is the twenty-first century—trying to create a country based solely on race is already an outdated way of thinking. It would be ridiculous to try and accomplish something with Sacred Blooded alone, and we would surely see limited results. We can only develop and evolve by doing away with exclusionism. The Holy Sacred Blood Empire is currently situated in the city of Oshiro along with our headquarters, but in time, we hope to see at least ten branches across the world create a coalition of the world's Sacred Blo— Shiren the First, please wake up. Her Majesty must stay awake."

Shiren had fallen asleep in the middle of the speech.

"*Yaaawn…* Oh! …I'm not asleep, I'm awake! I was listening!"

"Then summarize what I was talking about."

"Why do soba and ramen shops get so oddly particular about certain things? Sometimes, they ask you to take your first bite of soba without any sauce or start by sipping the ramen's broth. But isn't that up to the customer? Sure, it's fine to suggest those things, but it's outrageous to force people to do them. They clearly don't understand cuisine. One's meals should be free. That's what you were talking about."

"Exactly," Sairi replied sarcastically. As she thought, Shiren hadn't been listening at all—and her apparent pride was irritating.

"All right, now we'll have a very funny word from Shiren the First,

©Hiroki Ozaki

emperor of the Holy Sacred Blood Empire. You will surely find yourself rolling on the floor afterward! Be careful not to die of laughter! The comedy world will be changing right here, right now, tonight! Please give Her Majesty a round of applause!"

An earsplitting applause erupted throughout the room.

"Wait, hold on! You can't raise the stakes like that!" Shiren protested.

"Hmph! That's what you get for not listening to your mother." Sairi pouted.

With no other choice, Shiren took the stage.

"Uhh, I'm the emperor. Anyone got a problem with that?"

Her speech was disquieting right from the beginning.

"I want to govern the Sacred Blooded of the world to make sure we can all eat our fill. In fact, that is my only goal. Because when we starve, we are unable to do anything else. Both rich and poor live in this world. That is unavoidable. A world where everyone is rich is probably, like, theoretically impossible or something. But we cannot allow people to starve. When one has no food, one loses the ability to think of others. That leads to poverty of the soul. A lack of nutrients also makes one more prone to illness. To put it another way, if we all eat our fill, we will have energy to spare. That will give us more chances to live a fun and fulfilling life. We will be nicer to others. So our foremost goal is food. Food, food, food, food. Four square meals a day. With a full stomach, everything will work out. Food first!"

Shiren had no idea what she was supposed to talk about, so she said whatever came to mind. She was perfectly aware that this probably wasn't a very good speech, but she had to say something.

"The brainiacs can handle the diplomacy and negotiations and all that other boring stuff. I will govern on my ideals. An emperor does not conduct business—she rules. Anyone got a problem with that?"

""""Ohhh!""""

A cheer rose up from the crowd

"Way more riveting than I thought it'd be!" "I was expecting literally nothing, so that was infinitely better than I expected!" "Long live the emperor!" "In a way, that *was* pretty funny!"

It went over much better than either of them had expected.

"That was great, Shiren," Sairi said. "I guess you gave it serious thought in your own way."

"I didn't so much think about it as just say whatever came to mind…"

"Thank you, Shiren. This makes me very happy." Sairi offered a genuine smile. "You've grown so much. I'm bursting with joy."

"Oh, please. You're exaggerating."

"I'm still worried about your awful test scores, though."

"Please just forget about that!"

"Name five of Natsume Soseki's novels."

"*Ten Nights of Drinks, The Minor, I Am a Catdog, Then What?, The Body Pillow*."

"I'd kind of like to read *I Am a Catdog*."

"It's a romance novel about a dog who thinks he's a cat and ends up pining after a lady cat he can never be with."

"You're close with those titles, but you got all of them wrong. Keep studying." Sairi beamed with glee, delighting Shiren.

She was certain that Sairi had never smiled so much, so brightly, while the two of them were separated.

I think I could live my life for her…

Here, in the Holy Sacred Blood Empire. No matter what happens.

But even so, Shiren felt something was missing. There was something she would never have for herself at this rate.

I don't need to think about that.

She pushed those thoughts away. Her instinct told her one thing: Once she started down that road, there would be no turning back.

Characters

Kiyomizu Jouryuuji

Ryouta's classmate from school in Japan, as well as his stalker. She followed him into the Sacred Blood Empire. Assassin for the Virginal Father.

Tamaki Shijou

Classmate of Shiren and Ryouta. She's typically calm and collected, but once she slips into a pessimistic mood, there's no coming back for a while.

Sasara Tatsunami

A personal guard for the emperor, Ouka. She is madly in love with her liege and will often act recklessly because of it.

EPISODE 1
LET'S ENJOY OUR NEW LIVES!

Even though another Sacred Blooded nation had popped up in Japan, the lives of the people living in the Sacred Blood Empire remained unaffected.

On the surface, nothing had changed. It wasn't like any of the stores were being looted or glass was being broken and scattered everywhere. If they didn't watch TV, some might not even be aware anything was going on.

Freshmart Warakia was having its weekly sale, and a certain convenience store was selling an excess number of *Kairakuten* magazines. Even the day after a festival, with its lingering atmosphere of celebration, felt more unusual than this.

But just beneath the surface, things were not as easygoing.

In the First Cathedral, Alfoncina was engaged in yet another top secret phone call.

"Uh-huh~. So they weren't told at all? Mm-hmm~. So the Ministry of Foreign Affairs has split into two factions, and your rival faction is making progress. I see~."

There was a stern look on her face as she spoke into the mouthpiece. Her cheeks occasionally puffed out with discontent.

"That's what I'm saying. *Sorry, I didn't know* isn't going to cut it. They created their *own* country! Now *we* have to figure out how we're going to deal with it. And they used the Alfoncina name, which is going to be terrible for business! My real name? I would never! You know it's Matsuko Kimura, right? That name doesn't have an ounce of dignity!"

Alfoncina realized her voice was growing very sharp. Those who engaged in politics weren't supposed to let this much emotion show. Letting everyone on the other side of the table know exactly how she felt didn't make for good diplomacy.

But Alfoncina felt that she had been deceived, too. She had known there were some, maybe even a lot of Sacred Blooded who did not take kindly to their country.

That was inevitable, considering a small few professed to be the only ones representing the Sacred Blooded. They would, of course, make enemies of all those who were not happy with their methods.

Regardless, they still had to create the framework of what it meant to be Sacred Blooded. That was the price they had to pay for being first.

That said, it was almost impossible for a second Sacred Blooded nation to establish itself.

Ever since the Empire was founded in Akinomiya, she had heard the police had tightened up security and were being more cautious, and that was true. Japan would collapse if everyone and their grandmother started establishing countries for themselves, so the Japanese government was doing its best to prevent that from happening again.

And Alfoncina herself had leaked information to Japan about influential Sacred Blooded who were not on their side. Independence by the Sacred Blooded posed an even greater threat to the Empire than Japan.

So even if there was opposition, they should not have been able to accomplish anything. Alfoncina had been convinced of that.

But Sairi Fuyukura had managed to create another nation without direct help from Japan, and she had pulled it off by calling her group a "nation" in name only.

As a result, there had been no need for an uprising; it had been difficult to foresee, and she hadn't required that many backers. It wasn't against the law to begin with, so there was no way the government could have clamped down on it.

Not only that, but Sairi had also managed to establish both secular and religious aspects of this new nation by creating both an emperor *and* an archbishop.

There was no way to tell how many "citizens" she had without any real territory. Instead, however, they had a clear grasp on their institution's number of "supporters."

She might even be plotting to destroy our empire…

Once that thought took seed in Alfoncina's mind, she began to doubt everything.

Did Sairi take the name of Alfoncina because she was planning on over-shadowing her and tormenting her until she died?

Ouka is going to be smitten with Ryouta for a while, so she'll be useless. I suppose I must take matters into my own hands…

Alfoncina felt impatient. She didn't have the tools for what she needed to do.

I need to look into this now—their organization wasn't on our radar, and I don't have any useful connections… I knew we should have kept a closer eye on the Virginal Father… I didn't think the organization posed us any danger, but I had no idea it'd been weakened to that point.

What could she do? Alfoncina sank into her chair.

As she found herself at a loss for how to proceed, there came a knock at the door.

She could tell who it was right away by the knock—the secretary, one of her minions.

About ten of Alfoncina's minions worked at the First Cathedral. The one she trusted most among them was her secretary. Unfortunately, the woman had one habit Alfoncina absolutely hated.

"Um, Archbishop Kimura, a call came in for headquarters…"

Alfoncina did not budge. She sat still, leaning back in her chair.

"Considering the nature of the call, I wanted to come and confirm with you directly rather than send it on through the internal line…"

Alfoncina still did not turn around.

"Um……… Archbishop Alfoncina?"

"What is it?"

Alfoncina finally turned around. As always, she had zero intention of answering to her real name.

Her secretary always called her Kimura, which never failed to irritate Alfoncina. She really wished this woman would learn how to address people properly.

"Who is it from? It can't be my manga editor if they're calling for headquarters."

"It's from someone calling themselves New Progenitor Alfoncina…"

With a loud *clatter*, Alfoncina shot up from her chair.

"Transfer the call to me right now!"

Her heart was pounding in her ears. She took a deep breath before lifting the receiver so the person on the other end wouldn't know how flustered she was.

Her gaze sharpened and grew in intensity—this expression was for work only. No one at school had ever seen her like this before.

She readied a notepad and took a pen in her hand. If anything happened, she would write it down right away.

"Hello, this is Sairi Fuyukura, New Progenitor Alfoncina."

"Using that name—not that *I* have sole legal rights to it or anything—is a declaration that you intend to rival me, isn't it?"

"Rivalry? Are you implying war? I have no such intention. But it's good I called."

Alfoncina was doing everything in her power to read the emotion in Sairi's voice, but she could not sense any ulterior motives.

"Many, like you, think I'm being antagonistic. The reason I'm calling today is to explain myself, to let you know that isn't the case."

Sairi plainly denied any aggression on her part, but Alfoncina wasn't the type to naively celebrate prematurely. One's words and one's true intentions were different matters. She needed to confirm Sairi was expressing the latter and not the former.

She had already pressed the button to record their conversation. Depending on what happened, she might want to listen back for confirmation on one thing or another.

I will not give up on this country. I refuse to let Ouka's hard work go to waste.

She decided to ask her question first before Sairi could steal the initiative.

"If you have no intention of fighting, perhaps you can explain the reasoning behind this new country of yours?"

"People who aren't Sacred Blooded will find greater peace of mind with the birth of the Holy Sacred Blood Empire. I think this will benefit all Sacred Blooded."

©Hiroki Ozaki

"Peace of mind?"

"Yes. What I am hoping for is a revitalization of the Sacred Blooded." Sairi paused, briefly waiting for any response from Alfoncina, before continuing, "Until this moment, there has only been one country representing the Sacred Blooded. And this left regular humans anxious. They didn't know who the Sacred Blooded were or what they were thinking. Of course they were uneasy—they had nothing to compare any of that to. That unease will turn to fear, which will bring about persecution. You will find similar situations happening over and over again if you flip through any history book."

"So you created something to serve as a comparison, then...?"

"Yes. Having two separate camps will make it infinitely easier for others to determine what sort of people the Sacred Blooded are. Don't you think that will deepen their understanding of us? Perhaps our existence is a thorn in your side, but the best thing for the survival of the Sacred Blooded is to have another visible entity besides Akinomiya. We'll behave ourselves out here in Japan; that way, the Japanese people will feel as though they've domesticated the Sacred Blooded. I'm sure you understand that, Archbishop."

Alfoncina chuckled, but her laugh betrayed none of her emotion.

"I am perfectly clear on what you mean. I won't deny the benefits of having another 'empire' in Oshiro."

"I'm glad you understand."

"But that cannot be how you truly feel, can it?"

Alfoncina sensed Sairi's outward excuses and inward intentions were still jumbled.

"Oh my. You think I'm hiding something, don't you?"

"Perhaps having an opposing camp will ultimately prove beneficial. But no one would try to create another country entirely to those ends."

No person in their right mind would attempt something so tedious for such a roundabout reason. Sairi's words were almost certainly excuses. A real founder wouldn't use such rhetoric, nor would they act on such abstract ideals.

"You just wanted to create your own country, didn't you?"

Alfoncina could hear Sairi laughing on the other end.

Perhaps it was a given, considering they were speaking over the phone, but her voice sounded very far away.

Alfoncina returned the favor with an insincere laugh of her own. It was much easier to hide her intentions with a laugh than with anger.

But despite her smile, her eyes were cold. This was not funny at all. This was war.

"I would appreciate if you would stop laughing and answer my question."

"You're shrewd, Your Excellency."

"I'd rather not hear such a thing from you, Progenitor."

"Then I'll give you the truth, as a treat. I…wanted to give Shiren a country."

Alfoncina found herself nodding unconsciously. She now had her answer.

"I have put Shiren through so much pain and hardship up till now, including when I took her back. And I plan to give her everything to which she has a right."

"And one of those things is a country."

"Yes. She has the right to be emperor, you see."

"I do. I understand everything now."

With her free hand, Alfoncina wrote down a single note: "Blind parental love."

The pen slid easily across the paper.

Had Shiren ever even said she wanted those things?

"I will make up for every one of Shiren's lost opportunities. With this country, I can do that—I can give her everything. Things would be difficult if the country broke down, however, so I aim to make it something relatively durable. Well, you get the gist of it, I suppose. I have no ill will toward you all in Akinomiya, so rest easy."

The expression *you all in Akinomiya* touched a nerve, but Alfoncina ignored it.

"Shiren will have everything over here, and I mean everything. *We don't need the old Empire anymore. That place will only make her sad."*

And that was that.

Alfoncina now thoroughly understood Sairi's intentions, and it seemed safe to believe she would not attack them head-on. She was also impressed the other woman didn't suggest anything irritatingly optimistic such as the two empires remaining on good terms.

But there was one thing that still didn't sit right with her.

Emotions aside, there was nothing wrong with the situation. Alfoncina could have even shaken on it with a smile.

But I have a heart, too, you know.

She managed to keep herself from clicking her tongue, at least.

"I've heard what you had to say. I can see you have thought very hard about Shiren's happiness."

"That's because I've made her unhappy for a very long time."

"But the way you are doing things now will not make her happy. Thinking about making her happy and *actually* making her happy are two different things."

"...Why do you think that?"

"You're her mother. Think for yourself."

Alfoncina added another note to her pad: "Idiot."

She was starting to doubt that being a parent had anything to do with it.

Alfoncina was finding it difficult to pass this off with a smile. If she had been in the same room as Sairi, she would have been inclined to start lecturing her right then and there. Though perhaps it wouldn't mean anything coming from someone else.

"That is your duty as a mother, Progenitor."

Alfoncina did not wait for a response before hanging up. She sighed.

"I guess I need to be a better person, too."

She added another note to her pad: "Blind, doting, stupid parents will destroy their children."

She was starting to feel bad for Shiren. There were some things only a mother could give to her child. She had no doubt about that. But those things were only a tiny, tiny part of life.

It was the fourth night since the founding of the Holy Sacred Blood Empire.

Work had gone much more smoothly that day. There were a lot of documents, but Shiren had gotten a lot faster at stamping things now.

Sairi still had a lot to do and wouldn't be home for a while yet, so Shiren ate her buffet dinner alone.

Afterward, she decided to laze around in her room until her mother returned.

The bed in their hotel room was so soft and fluffy. She lay on top of it reading manga. There was an entire stack of unread volumes by her pillow, all of which she'd bought after leaving the Empire and coming to Japan.

Sairi had given her tens of thousands of yen just to buy manga, so it would be a while before she ran out. As a result, she'd managed to buy every volume of all the series she wanted, even those she'd been eyeing for a while but had been hesitant to start due to the massive backlog.

Sitting by the pile of manga was a box of expensive cookies. Every so often, she would take a break from reading to pop one in her mouth.

These cookies were one of the gifts they had received from various affiliates to celebrate the founding of the Holy Sacred Blood Empire. There had to be over a hundred boxes of just snacks and sweets. Even Shiren wasn't going to be finishing them for a while yet.

"Mm, it's a whole new experience reading *YouRou IKou!* in this country. I'd heard the volumes came with special goodies when you bought them in Japan, and it's true! But why don't they come with anything special in their original country? Oh, I suppose it's like when overseas CDs include special bonus tracks only on the Japanese editions. Maybe that's just the way things are."

Manga to enjoy.

A beautiful room.

Delicious treats.

In all honesty, compared with the dingy house she'd had in the Empire, this was like another world.

"Maybe this really is heaven. At least, actual heaven must be a lot like this. The most virtuous of people get to read all the manga they want, eat all the sweets they want, and live in fancy rooms like this one. People who hate manga go to hell."

She was so used to a commoner's life that even her ideas were cheap.

"And Mom is here, so everything is perfect—as perfect as a dish of avocado, tuna, and wasabi soy sauce."

"You sure talk to yourself a lot."

It was then that Shiren realized Kiyomizu was standing by the window. She was wearing loose ninja clothes that allowed her to move freely; this was probably a combat outfit.

It didn't seem like she'd come to hang out, and she looked a little fed up. Shiren could easily believe the girl was here to assassinate her.

Shiren sat up on her bed; it wasn't easy to talk while lying down.

"Hey, you know this is the thirty-fifth floor, right...? How did you get in...?"

"The window."

"I thought I closed the window."

The window was, in fact, open. This was a skyscraper, so strong gusts of wind were blowing in.

"I used Virginal Father techniques," Kiyomizu replied.

"Aren't those abilities of yours a little too overpowered? They're basically cheating."

"Do not underestimate the order of the Virginal Father. For me, there is no such thing as a locked door. A room dozens of stories above ground is the same as a one-story building. The prime minister's official residence and the Diet Building are but houses made of straw."

In essence, she could get into any place she wanted.

"What do you want, then? Ryouta isn't here, so— Oh."

The moment the words left her mouth, she realized what had been bothering her. She'd been trying so hard this whole time not to think about Ryouta, and now...

"Forget Ryouta dearest for today. When I heard you'd become emperor of a weird little country, I decided to drop by and tease you on my way home."

"No need to trouble yourself. My life is so utterly and perfectly fulfilled right now that nothing you do could possibly bother me." Shiren folded her arms and turned her head away.

Who does this intruder think she is? No one in the new Empire had said anything so ridiculous to her. Everyone here merely sang her praises as the emperor.

"I thought you might say that."

"Then wallow in your envy of my amazing new life and be on your way. You can take a box of sweets if you want, too. I'm generous, you see."

Kiyomizu surveyed the hotel room.

"Mm. Your standard of living has shot through the roof—it's almost comical. Even a tenfold income increase wouldn't normally result in this kind of life. And though this might be a bit rude to my dearest Ryouta, your previous life was a bit of a joke, as well."

"Exactly. I'm an emperor now. I'm important—important enough to eat every dish at the hotel buffet every single day. And I do just that."

She was definitely overeating.

"I don't have to check for special-deal days at Freshmart Warakia anymore. I don't have to choose the cheapest butter or miso anymore."

"You're still thinking like a commoner."

"That'll go away as time passes, I think… Anyway, right now, everything is super great. That's all there is to it."

"You sure look bored considering things are 'super great,'" Kiyomizu replied, as if stating the obvious. Her expression hadn't changed since she arrived.

Everything was just as she'd predicted. Shiren wasn't enjoying her life here at all.

"Th-that's not true! How could any lifestyle be richer or more fulfilling than this? And didn't I just say? My life is totally perfect right now!"

"To be honest, it hurts to look at you right now. Like watching someone in the pits of hell."

"Where on Earth did that come from?! This isn't hell—this is heaven!"

"Whatever. But I do have one thing to say to you."

"What…?"

"Those who can't even figure out what makes them happy are the biggest idiots of all."

Kiyomizu's gaze was now full of scorn. She seemed to sense nothing she said would get through to the other girl.

©Hiroki Ozaki

"I'm not stupid…"

"What grade did you get on your last world-history test, then?"

"Two percent."

"Your stupidity is of historic proportions."

"I mean, I was planning on living my entire life in the Sacred Blood Empire, so I didn't think I needed to know any world history…"

"And then you left everyone in the Empire behind."

"No, I didn't!" Shiren retorted loudly.

You don't even know what kind of position I was in, she thought.

"I didn't have a choice! What else was I supposed to do?! This was the only way to make everyone happy!"

She couldn't leave Sairi by herself, and she couldn't keep Ryouta from Ouka any longer. She felt guilty—she had already taken so much from her sister.

"'No other choice,' huh? Doesn't that mean this isn't what you really want?"

Shiren's shoulders suddenly drooped.

"It's not fair to ask leading questions like that…"

"That was not my intention; you merely revealed your true feelings. If I really wanted to draw the truth out of you, I would use the order's truth serum."

"I guess it's impossible to keep your feelings hidden forever…," Shiren whimpered. She had been trying to play it off, but Kiyomizu saw right through her. "I had no idea it'd be so hard not being able to see everyone."

She couldn't say a word of this to Sairi or any of the other important people in the organization, but she could be honest with Kiyomizu.

She had everything in the new Empire—everything that could be obtained with money, at least. She could spoil herself rotten if she wanted.

But her friends were all gone.

"I mean, I knew it'd be lonely. But imagining it and actually feeling it are two entirely different things. I can't believe how stupid I am, noticing only after it's too late… Ryouta, Big Sis, Tamaki, Alfoncina, Sasara, Kokoko…"

"You completely skipped over dearest Ryouta's sister."

"Oh, Rei! I forgot about her! Sorry, Rei! I didn't mean anything bad by it. I probably just skipped over my tutor because I don't want to study. I didn't forget anyone else, did I? …I think I'm safe…"

Shiren was conscientious about the strangest things.

"If I'd known at the beginning how tough it would be without everyone around, I might not have chosen this path…"

But it was too late. Her only choice now was to live out her life in the Holy Sacred Blood Empire.

"Or maybe that still wouldn't have stopped me… Maybe nothing would have changed…"

"What makes you say that?"

"This is where my mom is."

It didn't matter whether she found herself in heaven or hell after leaving the Sacred Blood Empire. Wherever Sairi was, that's where she had to go. She couldn't leave her mother alone, even if that meant she couldn't take anyone else with her.

Because otherwise, Sairi would be alone.

Shiren was the only person on the planet who could save her. Ryouta might find happiness with Ouka, but no one could take Shiren's place when it came to her mother.

"Did your mother ever bother to contact you before, though? Even my own idiot of a father sends me a text every once in a while."

"Ryouta did everything he could to help me when I was alone, even though he got nothing out of it."

Shiren turned to look out the window. She had never noticed it before, but there was a point in the distance where the night lights abruptly grew sparse. Beyond that was darkness. At the edge of Oshiro lay the mountains—no one lived there. And even farther away was the old city of Akinomiya—the old Sacred Blood Empire.

"So I felt like I had an obligation to help my mom, too. I'd be the worst person ever if I didn't…" Putting it into words was helping her feel a little better. "I had to. This is my fate. I might be a bit lonely, but I'll just have to endure. I'm not a kid anymore, you know. I'll get through it, you'll see."

Shiren's expression finally relaxed. After all, Sairi would be hurt if she saw her daughter sad all the time. She would find the energy to keep going here. That was her mission.

But—

"You're way more of an idiot than I thought," Kiyomizu said, apparently disappointed.

"Why?! Shouldn't you compliment me for having my heart in the right place or something?! There's no crying over spilled milk, so I'm not gonna cry!"

Shiren was angry that her decision had been so easily denied.

"If you've already decided for yourself that it's all in the past, then there's no helping you."

"But shouldn't an adult know when to give up…? That's the only thing you can do in the face of the impossible, right?"

"You still have plenty of time to change your course, and giving up before you can even try is just running away from your problems."

"Whatever! I'll do things my own—"

"I can't believe you're the same woman who made Ryouta dearest her minion!"

Shiren froze at Kiyomizu's words. Her legs faltered, and she came to sit at the desk. Her mouth opened slightly, but no sound came out.

"'The impossible'? Do you not remember how many times *he* ran up against the impossible only to overcome it?"

"Stop talking about Ryouta…"

"No matter what happened, he never gave up. No matter how hard the battle, he kept trying. I am most certain we saw the same thing, didn't we? Weren't you always right by his side?"

"……"

"If Ryouta dearest gave up as easily as you have now, then you would have stayed alone forever! You are an idiot who never learns!"

Kiyomizu slammed her hand onto the desk loud enough to echo in the room. Then she moved her hand away to reveal a piece of notebook paper. On the paper was a string of ten numbers.

"That number connects to the office of an executive in your organization.

If you ever want to go home, just give them a call and let them hear how you really feel. Regular phone calls from Japan don't connect to the old Empire anymore, you see. You'll have to seek help from Japan first."

"Have you wormed your way into the new Empire, too?"

"That's not for you to know. You just have to do what you can with what you have. Well, whether you *do* anything or not is entirely up to you."

Kiyomizu had begun to speak faster. It seemed like she was rapidly running out of time.

Shiren silently picked up the piece of paper. Why did something so light feel so heavy?

"But…if you don't act fast, it really will be too late."

Kiyomizu, her expression still cold, turned to exit from the window.

"Hey, this is the thirty-fifth floor… It's a lot higher than the stage of Kiyomizu Temple, and the survival rate is probably a lot lower…"

"The *stage of Kiyomizu Temple*? Such a trifle is hardly tall enough to serve the needs of the order of the Virginal Father's elite."

That was all Kiyomizu said before vanishing from the balcony.

With nothing to obstruct it, the night breeze now washed over Shiren.

The air in Oshiro felt much colder than that of the old Empire, maybe because she was high up in a skyscraper. The wind was uncomfortably strong.

The city below shone much brighter than any sight in her old home, but for some reason, it felt colder, bleaker.

She had everything, yet she felt something lacking. No, it didn't just *feel* like it—it was true. Something was missing.

"I think it might take me a while to get used to this life…"

How long would it take before that feeling went away? The thought scared her, and she didn't want to think about it.

"I'm really bad at using my brain… That's why I don't want to do the math…"

Just then, she heard the door open.

"I'm home, Shiren. Work's finally over."

Sairi, dressed in a suit, stepped inside with a friendly look on her face. This was her home, too, of course.

"You opened the window. Did something happen?" Sairi asked. "You look tired."

Sairi, on the other hand, seemed to radiate joy. She had built her own country and was now enjoying life with Shiren. Her expression was the exact opposite of her daughter's.

"It's nothing important," Shiren said, slowly shaking her head.

"Are you sure? You can talk to me if something's bothering you."

"I know, Mom."

But she could never tell her this. It wasn't a desire Sairi could fulfill, after all.

"I know this is so incredibly rude of me to ask, Ryouta, but there is something I have been wondering for quite a while now. If afterward you can't forgive me, please feel free to punch or kick me. My third father often punched me... Oh, that's right, I don't need to call him Father anymore. Oh, I'm sorry, you don't care about my personal life, do you? Not even the counselor at the help center was interested in that. I'm here to talk about you... Are you awake?"

"......"

"No answer. But you're not a corpse, right...? No corpse could ever sit so naturally in a chair. Goodness, is this rigor mortis? Have you been poisoned? But no one has a grudge against you, unlike me. Actually, I don't think anyone holds a grudge against me, either. After all, once they see my pitiful life, how could they begrudge me? I am powerless, and thus, I am harmless. So long as I don't consider existence itself to be a punishment, I should be all right. Ha-ha-ha... More importantly, why were *you* killed...?"

"Oh, Shijou? I'm alive, actually."

"I thought I heard a voice. But it could be an auditory hallucination. When we started to find ourselves strapped for money at the store, I often thought I heard customers, even though the store was supposedly empty. I could be having a relapse..."

"You're not hallucinating! Don't worry!"

"But you've been like an empty husk this whole time, so I was worried... Your eyes have gone blank ever since lunch."

Ryouta was vaguely aware that Tamaki was correct. Ever since Shiren left, he'd had a hard time focusing at school. He would absently listen to his classes, then suddenly find the day was over.

He had a feeling things would change if Ouka talked to him, but ever since they'd told each other how they felt, she scarcely spoke to him in class, even though she sat right next to him.

Just then, Ouka was debating with Sasara about how to create a system of government that would garner them more support the more they raised taxes.

"I believe the people won't feel that something is being taken from them if we provide them something tangible in exchange for the tax increase."

"They may stop feeling grateful after a while, but we might be able to trick them a few times. What do you propose we give them?"

"I was thinking your used—"

"All right, I know what the next word is, so you can stop right there. Now, I was considering approving a bill that would force a marriage between the Tatsunami and Toraha households."

"Oh, Lady Ouka, I am so sorry! Please forgive me!"

"Then come up with a real idea. I don't want to lose any more support."

"I doubt your support could fall any lower."

"The Tatsunami-Toraha Compulsory Marriage Bill—"

"Please stop!" Sasara did not want that bill to become a law. "Well...I understand how important taxes are, but it appears you haven't spoken to any nearby classmates in some time... Perhaps you should work on your interpersonal communication..."

"Nearby classmates? Oh, I see what you mean." Ouka's gaze drifted to Ryouta, then returned to Sasara. "It's fine. I can talk to him however much I like when we get home."

Ryouta heard her remark loud and clear. He was sitting right next to her, after all.

We've basically been living together, so maybe she's embarrassed... That makes perfect sense.

When he thought about it logically, their current arrangement was outrageous for a pair of high schoolers. Some of their classmates were even starting to spread rumors.

But though they lived together, their lives were very chaste and wholesome. They lived in the same apartment and slept in the same bed, but they kept to opposite sides.

He was nervous, of course, and often found himself hyperaware of her presence, but that was it. They each knew how the other felt, but their relationship didn't seem likely to progress beyond that. There was nothing to push them any further.

But Ryouta was happy. He almost couldn't believe he was living under the same roof as Ouka.

I must keep spacing out because I'm so happy. I'll just think of it that way…

"You're off in la-la land again, Ryouta. Oh, I'm sorry I keep talking to you. I don't have any friends, so you're the only one I can really talk to… I suppose I could just talk to a wall, though, couldn't I? But it's true I'm worried about you…"

"Yeah, I guess."

"Is your brain even working…?"

"Yeah, I guess."

"Then you wouldn't mind if I sent you a thousand frozen jam rolls, right?"

"Yeah, I guess."

"All right. I'll put in an order."

The following day, Ryouta would be totally baffled when a thousand jam rolls arrived in the mail, but that's another story for another time.

Nothing much was going on in class. The day felt pretty laid-back, even putting aside Ryouta's circumstances.

But just then, a force from outside ripped that atmosphere to shreds.

Come here, come here, I have something very important to tell you, so come here, come here, come here. They say seeing is believing, so come here, come, come, come.

*   *   *

He heard a voice pleading profusely inside his head.

Ryouta abruptly stood up from his seat.

"Oh! Goodness, what is it? Have I spoken to you too much and now you've had enough of me? Y-you may hit me if you like, but I would rather you not leave any marks on my face, so please hit my arms or legs if you can... Oh, that's not to say my face is particularly pretty or that injuring it would really change anything, ha-ha-ha..."

Tamaki was always rather dispirited, but Ryouta's sudden movement had startled her a little.

"Sorry, Shijou. I need to go! Move! Watch out!"

"Eep!"

Ryouta pushed Tamaki aside as the invisible force pulled him forward, and he dashed out of the classroom. She had been in his way, and he wasn't fully in control.

"I'm really sorry, Shijou!"

He glanced back at her as she fell on her rear and apologized. His legs didn't seem like they were going to stop.

"Oh, I've been punished... But I suppose I should be thankful it isn't any worse... For an entire half an hour, my third father would... No, I shouldn't speak ill of the dead. I should keep silent..."

Ryouta could faintly hear Tamaki's words—gloomy in both tone and content—as he rushed down the hallway.

No one in class, however, was listening to her.

The invisible force pushed—or rather, pulled—Ryouta all the way up the stairs and to the roof.

"*Huff, huff, huff...* Could you be a little gentler calling me...?"

Just as he'd thought, Alfoncina was waiting for him on the roof.

She was leaning over the fence, gazing at the athletic fields below. For some reason, she was out of uniform and wearing the modified priestess outfit indicating her status as archbishop.

"It seems a bit of my power remains within you~. Even though you're now officially Ouka's minion."

"It isn't like our connection gets overwritten. Still, you really shouldn't do this, because I *am* Ouka's minion now."

"There's no rule outlawing the summoning of those who aren't our minions. On the contrary, I'd say this is proof that the connection between master and minion isn't as firm as it should be."

"And that's why I'm asking you to stop."

Ouka would not be happy if she found out. And if it soured her mood, the one who suffered the brunt of it would be Ryouta. They shared a room, after all.

"Well-, to be honest, even I thought summoning you was going a bit too far. Tee-hee."

Ryouta couldn't see Alfoncina's expression, but he knew there was a bitter smile on her face.

"Ouka's in your class, though, so I wouldn't be able to have a genuine chat with you there. I couldn't say that one's master should be fluid."

"What do you mean?"

Alfoncina kept her gaze trained out toward the fields. It was easier for Ryouta to speak face-to-face. He was having a hard time reading her this way.

"You don't get it?"

"I don't."

"What I *mean* is that if you see someone you consider your master in trouble, you should help them."

Suddenly, Alfoncina whirled around to face him, grabbing both of his hands. Her palms were awfully warm, and the expression on her face was just as heated.

"Uh, Alfoncina? What are you—?"

"Ouka did all she could to make things go her way, didn't she? But she can only push so far. Once two people settle into a relationship, no official minionship can do much to change that."

Alfoncina's face was flushed. Heat was coursing through her blood vessels and spreading to every corner of her body. Ryouta could tell from where her hands were holding his.

"You're being really forward... Isn't this kind of out of character for you?"

"Perhaps. You may have seen similar comments about the recent chapters of *YouRou IKou!* It was supposed to be a fun comedy manga, but the characters are starting to get serious. Some people think I'm going too far."

Ryouta, too, was vaguely aware of this change in her manga. The switch-up in and of itself was kind of fun, but now things were going in a different direction than before. It was probably hard to accept for the fans who just wanted more low-key jokes and gags.

"It happens. It's kind of like when an author popular for their erotic manga starts up a new story with a serious narrative, and the fans keep asking to see more skin."

"Yes, I suppose that does happen. But in most cases, the author isn't doing it simply to try something new."

"Oh?"

For some reason, Alfoncina puffed out her chest with pride as she spoke.

"Most times, that new work turns out to be the thing the creator *actually* wanted to create, to express—it might even be a reflection of their genuine feelings."

"I guess you really are a pro, Hayashimori," Ryouta replied. "That makes total sense..."

Ryouta leaned back a little as he looked at Alfoncina's face. She was way too close to him.

His impression of her was that she was always several paces away, grinning at him. But now she was very close, physically *and* emotionally.

"I hope you'll keep supporting Kin Hayashimori in the future."

"O-of course... I'll keep reading the manga."

"But right now, I'm here as Alfoncina the Thirteenth, doing the archbishop's job."

"Your job...? What, you mean bringing all the Sacred Blooded together...?"

"To make my believers smile," she said, beaming. "I wish I could live a more relaxed life, but sometimes, that's just not in the cards."

She wasn't being very specific, but Ryouta understood the gist of what she was trying to say.

"I'm sure Shiren's living a happy life out there, Alfoncina." Shiren had chosen to live in a world with Sairi. He'd been reluctant to part with her, but he had to respect her decision. "After all, only Shiren can decide how she lives her life…"

He could clearly see Alfoncina's pupils shrink to pinpricks. She pinched the skin on his hands.

"Owww! No violence, please! And how do you know just where to pinch so it really hurts?! No one else has ever caused me that much pain with a single pinch!"

Alfoncina's expression remained calm, as though she was in the middle of taking a test.

"You don't know how much it pains me to hurt you."

"That's obviously not true… Whoa, wait, I remember seeing this in *You-Rou IKou!*… Rouko did this to someone…"

Rouko had pinched Kouko and said the exact same thing. Then Kouko had yelled, "Not as much as it pains me!"

"You're a real idiot, Ryouta. This is going way beyond a personality trait. You're actually hurting people."

"What are you talking about…? And can you stop pinching me, please…?"

"Did you see Shiren happy with your own two eyes?"

"Well, no, but…"

Alfoncina stared hard at him.

"She's not with the person most important to her—there's no way she's happy."

Her words were powerful enough to make him feel dizzy.

"At least, we of the Holy Church of the Sacred Blood do not consider that to be happiness."

"But she has Sairi with her…"

"Do you think that's enough? Do you truly believe that?"

"P-probably…"

"Then I have one last question for you. Why have you been so spacey, Ryouta? Aren't you happy with your life with Ouka? Then why? Are you trying to hide something and failing? Do you honestly think you can go on as you always have? I doubt there's as much time left as you think there is. I've seen plenty of troubled people in my time as archbishop, and I know that if you don't act fast, you'll regret it later. People's hearts are delicate things. And once they've shriveled, there's no going back!"

Alfoncina wasn't asking questions anymore; she was simply spewing out her thoughts. And the shock of her words stirred up all the feelings in Ryouta's heart.

"............I'm sorry, Alfoncina." Everything he had tried to bury deep in his heart was bubbling to the surface. "But I still don't know what to do... She's so far away now... Literally."

The truth was that this boundary wouldn't be easy to cross. Still, part of him was panicking—he couldn't just leave things the way they were. And that panic was steadily growing, even if he didn't notice it.

"All right," Alfoncina said, lightly patting Ryouta's head. "You still have some time, so long as you've held on to your heart. Well, *you* have time, at least."

"Th-thank you..."

"No need to thank me. And I'm sorry for disturbing you."

Alfoncina smiled and moved to leave the rooftop. But before she left, she turned toward him one last time.

"Haah~. I really wish things would get rom-com-y again, like they used to be."

Her voice was too quiet to reach Ryouta. Still, she had said it out loud knowing full well he wouldn't hear.

"I wonder what he would've done if I'd said the wrong thing?" Alfoncina murmured, taking one step at a time down the stairs. "He really does have a thick skull."

At this point, she had no qualms or reservations saying how she felt about him. But she wasn't about to throw yet another spanner in the works—and besides, she was the archbishop. So she kept quiet.

"—I'll just leave it at that."

Characters

Alfoncina XIII

The archbishop of the Holy Church of the Sacred Blood who enjoys idol-like popularity throughout the Empire. She is a year above Ryouta and his classmates at school. Her real name is Matsuko Kimura.

Rei Asagiri

Ryouta's big sister. Her infatuation with her younger brother drove her to follow him to the Empire. She now works as a ninja for Ouka, the emperor.

Kokoko

The daughter of a god who had been enshrined in the Empire's mountains. She calls herself a fox, but she has rabbit ears. She works at Nine-to-Eleven, Tamaki's family's convenience store.

EPISODE 2
LET'S FORGE OUR OWN PATH!

Right about the time Alfoncina was pinching Ryouta's hand, something was happening in the old Empire's castle.

The castle staff had no idea, either, because it was taking place underground, on a floor regular people couldn't visit.

"I finally won... I finally beat them all... Putting so many hard games back-to-back has to be illegal... *Ehem, ehem.* Oh dear, I think playing so many video games has made my cough worse. *Ehem, ehem...*"

Rei stared at the ending credits on the TV screen with bloodshot eyes.

Security underground had been raised considerably ever since Sairi invaded.

An NES console with ten N*ntendo-hard games had been placed in the hallway—all titles that were universally panned for being too difficult. The door at the end of the hallway would not open unless you beat every one of them.

Not only that, but if one also got a game over at any point, they would be sent back to the very first game without any continues, even if they'd cleared several beforehand. And since the whole setup required forcing aged hardware to work again, the slightest external vibration meant the screen would glitch and freeze. It was a thoroughly brutal affair.

Rei, with all her bad luck, had experienced two freezes that resulted in a full restart. The second time was so upsetting, her heart had stopped for a bit, too.

"These old games are such a handful—a lot of them seem to place the emphasis on conquering a difficult system over actually enjoying the game... An unskilled player might end up throwing away a game they bought, unable to ever see the ending..."

The shutter behind the TV slowly rolled open.

"Now then, what sort of trial awaits me next?"

The next room had a computer in it. It seemed the computer was running a very old dating sim. The rules were taped to the wall: *Get the good ending for every girl, even the hidden characters.*

"This has got to be simpler than the last round. I don't think I'll have to concentrate as hard... Wait, there must be a catch..."

When she researched the game on her phone, she was met with a terrible verdict.

"Um, this says... 'One, affection mechanics in this game are incredibly harsh. If you pick the wrong choice even once, you won't trigger any events. Two, even if your affection level is high enough to trigger events, the most important events are triggered essentially at random, so if you have bad luck, you'll only get friend endings. Three, the game's story loops, but there's no skip function for either read or unread dialogue, so you have to read the same lines over and over again. Four, for some reason, your cursor will go straight to the first option when it's time to make a dialogue decision. I guess the devs thought they were being nice, but if you're just clicking to get through dialogue, you will accidently choose the first option every time. Five, there's one character whose events won't trigger unless you pick the nonsensical options, so you can't finish this game by choosing only the most logical responses. Six, there's a bug where the game freezes when you save, so you can't save scum. Seven, there's a bug where the game crashes depending on the option order, so you have to go through characters in a certain order. This is truly a garbage fire of a game'... Am I in for another hellish experience...?"

In the end, Rei's inherent bad luck came to a head, preventing her from triggering any events. It took her twenty hours to clear the game.

Once again, the shutter on the other side of the room rolled open.

"I finally...got through it... If I remember correctly, the next door should be a really tough one, like the kind on a bank vault."

She had no plan for how she was going to get through it, but she needed to in order to do her job.

"I won't let this stop me. I will not bend to any door or stupid, crappy game!"

The door in question had been sliced in two, and on it, she found a paper that read *UNDER CONSTRUCTION*.

"Oh, Sairi must have done this… I suppose she *is* very powerful. *Ehem, ehem…*"

The special door had been broken in a very special way, and it seemed repairs were going to take a while.

At the end of the passage, Rei came across a room decorated in an eerie fashion. The floor was carpeted with a rug that appeared to be covered in blood, and there were rose petals scattered across it. The curtains were drawn, despite the room being underground, and they had ominous designs on them featuring skulls and bats.

"I've come here countless times to deliver messages, but it never fails to give me goose bumps…"

This room, of course, belonged to Ouka's mother—Ominaeshi Sarano.

"Hello? Hello!" Rei knocked on the coffin in the middle of the room.

"How obnoxious! Can't you summon me in a quieter manner?!"

Wham!

The coffin flew open, and Ominaeshi emerged. As she did, the lid smashed into Rei, who went hurtling backward and landed on her head.

"Oh dear… I've done it again… Oh no, her skull has split, and *real* blood now colors my rug…! Hello! Please wake up! I only pretend to be a stereotypical vampire; I cannot handle the sight of so much blood!"

"This is nothing. It's not enough to kill me." Rei sat up, blood still pouring from her head.

"I simply cannot understand by what standard you are judging things. If you're really that tough, can you at least appear as if you're taking no damage? Watching you is bad for *my* heart."

Ominaeshi wore a black dress as always and was cooling herself off with a black fan.

"Sorry about that. If you don't mind, I've come to deliver a message. *Ehem, ehem.*"

"A message? From whom? I don't mean to brag, but I have very few friends."

Would that technically be a humblebrag?

"All right, allow me to recite the message: '……………Good luck.'"

"I need a little more information! Couldn't they have written what the good luck was *for*?!"

The message had been more abstract than expected.

"I'm sorry, but I forgot more and more of the message as the games held me up. I did remember that it was something encouraging, though…"

"Then at least tell me who it came from…"

"Hmm, what was the name again…?"

"You must be the least qualified messenger in existence… If you have nothing to tell me, then I am going back to sleep. I wish to spend every moment possible sleeping."

"Oh, I know!" Rei clapped her hands together. "Ms. Ominaeshi, I'll go back to sleep to confirm the message, **so could you please strangle me?**"

"By '*sleep*,' do you mean *eternal slumber*…? I would rather not have any brushes with the police… If it comes to that, I'll need to have my daughter use her Imperial power to forcibly erase all evidence."

"It's all right. I'm just going to the world with the flower field~."

"I have a feeling you may not be able to come back from such a world… but very well. I shall do as you ask!"

Ominaeshi wrapped her hands around Rei's throat.

(*DO NOT TRY THIS AT HOME.)

"Agh… Augh! Ah…ah… *Slump*."

Rei's head lolled to the side. She had lost consciousness.

"Now, what shall I do with her? I suppose I shall lay her down until she wakes up. But I do not want to put her in my coffin. That spot is for me alone. If she were to die for real, it would hinder my next slumber."

Ominaeshi was also aware of Rei's special qualities (?) and was not terribly bothered by the situation. She was not the cruel sort of person who would happily wring the neck of anyone who asked.

"Mm, I suppose I'll lay her down on the rug."

She wasn't very gentle.

Fifteen minutes later—

"*Phew*, the conversation got so involved that I almost missed the boat back home. *Ehem, ehem*. Had I missed it, I wouldn't have been able to come back... Close call!"

"The boat? That means you did pass into the next life for a moment... You have put yourself at risk."

"But I did find the person I was looking for, and we had a good chat."

"Oh, so you completed your mission?"

"We got really into talking about old NES JRPGs!"

"Do not pass into the afterlife simply to reminisce with people of your own generation!"

"We eventually agreed that *G*ga Z*mbie no Gy*kushu* is an essential title."

"I did not find it particularly impressive myself. I would say that's your nostalgia speaking. In terms of entertainment, while I know this is toward the latter half of that era, the *Goemon* RPGs..."

They spoke for half an hour.

"Everyone says it's the dodgeball that makes the series, but personally speaking, I preferred the soccer~."

"Oh, the one with hunter team versus the ninja team! You always had to use the really powerful teammates who could send the ball straight to the goal no matter where it ended up. Often, they'd knock the opposing goalie out of the way, too, giving you extra points. You could only block so many of the opponent's special shots, so it was nearly impossible to win by blocking. But isn't this a little before your time...? I'm starting to think you've given me the wrong age."

"I really like historical series, too! If you lower the difficulty just a touch, then all the enemies die in a single hit!"

"I think you are, indeed, lying about your age."

"No, I'm fourteen."

That would make her younger than Rei's own little brother.

"Oh. And what was that message you had for me?" asked Ominaeshi.

"I forgot."

*   *   *

(*She crossed into the afterlife once again.)

"I arrived when he was with another woman, and things got dicey. I thought I was going to die there, too! *Ehem, ehem...*"

"You're putting yourself on the line even more than a bad stand-up act... What was the message, then?"

"Yes, yes. I definitely remember this time. I just heard it, after all. It's still fresh in my mind."

Rei played the part of dependable messenger. She even imitated the sender's manner of speech, as if it was some sort of performance.

Because of that, the message took quite some time to say, and more and more tears began to well in Ominaeshi's eyes as she listened.

By the time Rei finished relaying the message, Ominaeshi's cheeks were stained with tears.

She did not even care that it was ruining her makeup.

"No... This isn't fair... Abusing the privileges of the dead... Pretending to be a good person in the next life... People only grow more beautiful in death... And after he was unreasonable and egotistical and a complete rascal in life!"

Ominaeshi sat on her coffin. She no longer had the energy to stand. Rei came to sit next to her.

"I'm glad I got to tell you."

She gently handed the other woman a handkerchief. Ominaeshi took it wordlessly.

When she brought it to her eyes, tears quickly came to wet it.

"To be honest, I thought it would be kind of a pain to go back and ask again; I considered just winging it so I didn't have to. It isn't as though anyone else could check. *Ehem, ehem.*"

"That's quite a statement to deliver so casually."

"An adult's life is difficult. The longer one lives, the more burdens one comes to shoulder."

"Yes, and I have been through so many terrible things already. I hope my life is filled with nothing but joy from here on out."

"Though, I think I might be a full twelve years younger than you."

"What a bold thing for a twentysomething to say! You will soon grow old! This is the only time you can get away with acting young!"

"I told you, I'm fourteen!"

"We both know that is a lie!"

"I know things are tough for us adults, but let's do what we can, okay? For the younger generations."

"I am forever seventeen."

In the end, Rei's bid for adult sympathy was denied.

"What? But you have to be at least twice my—"

"You will not finish that sentence, lest I wring your neck again."

Neither of them had an ounce of adult decorum.

"Still, we cannot inflict hardship on my daughter's generation. I don't wish them to inherit the consequences of our mistakes. To make them suffer simply because we did would only bring about senseless resentment..."

Ominaeshi stood and pulled back the creepy curtain on the wall. A framed picture hung behind it.

It was a picture of the day Ouka graduated from elementary school. On either side of her stood Ominaeshi and her late husband, Ouen.

One of them was gone now, but that was precisely why she had to live to her fullest to make sure Ouka was happy.

"There is...another to whom I would like for you to deliver the message. Will you do it?" Ominaeshi asked, her head lowered and her voice muffled. This was important, but it was still difficult to say out loud.

"Of course. I made it all the way to you. Anything else should be a cinch."

Rei took on the job without question.

"Thank you."

Ominaeshi then gave her the name of the other recipient.

"I had thought as much," Rei said. "It will be difficult, *ehem, ehem,* but I will do it. *Ehem, ehem.*"

"Yes. I wish you the best of luck. However"—a bleak look crossed Ominaeshi's face—"that does not mean everything will go back to how it used to be, nor do I intend to offer any assistance." She slowly pulled the curtain back across the painting. The framed photo was once again hidden from

©Hiroki Ozaki

view. "I want things to be better for the younger generation. But it is up to them to decide how they want to live. They must decide whether they want happiness or not."

Rei nodded slowly.

"While Ouka has lost Shiren, she has forged a new bond. No one can deny this fact. Real life cannot be reset with the press of a button as one does on the NES, no matter how much one wishes."

"Just now, you used the NES as a stand-in for all games, didn't you? I hate to break it to you, but most games don't have a button like that anymore."

"This is not the appropriate time for such a retort."

"I don't mind if things can't go back to how they were before. Even if they did, Ryou would only be attached at the hip to someone else who isn't me."

"You are his elder sister. There is nothing you can do about that."

"I will fight until the laws are amended! But…"

Rei looked up at the gaudy, low, gothic ceiling. It was hard to tell if it was the color choice or the design that made it seem so low.

"…it'd be even worse if Ryou was unhappy, and I have a feeling he won't find happiness like this. *Ehem, ehem.*"

I need to get out of here and look at the sky, she thought. This place was suffocating.

"Don't you ever go outside, Ominaeshi?"

As time passed after the establishment of the Holy Sacred Blood Empire, Shiren found rhythm in her new life.

In the morning, she would study with the tutor Sairi had hired. This tutor was a better teacher than Rei, but it was a bit awkward working with a stranger.

In the afternoon, she attended to her work as emperor. That said, all this "work" entailed was greeting guests who came to visit and stamping some documents.

She would eat dinner a little after six, then read manga in her hotel room. Then she would wait for Sairi to return.

"How strange… This is a very interesting manga, but I'm not enjoying myself at all… Is this room too fancy…? It must not be suited to manga-reading!"

Shiren tossed the manga away and sprawled across her bed. The soft mattress gently cradled her…sort of. Not really. No soft bed could soothe her discontent.

She wasn't sure what was wrong, what was missing.

"Maybe it's time I stop lying to myself…"

She knew the truth. And if she continued to brush it off, saying all she needed to do was be patient and endure, it would soon be too late. Time was quickly running out.

Her eyes snapped to the desk. She got up and quietly pulled open the drawer.

Though she knew what was inside, she still found her heart clenching when it entered her field of view. For some reason, she felt like she was doing something very wrong.

It was the note Kiyomizu had left with her—a dry, emotionless note, one that held only a telephone number. A number that might change her life.

She stared at the digits for a little while before closing the drawer.

This wasn't the time, not yet. There was an order to these things.

She couldn't go looking for help far away just yet. After all, she still had people she could rely on right by her side.

It was then that Sairi returned from work. Her crisp, creased suit flattered her—she truly looked the part of an executive.

"Welcome back, Mom."

"Goodness~. It seems there was a little incident with an intruder. The new order of the Virginal Father was thrown into chaos because of it, though it seems they successfully sent her packing."

"An intruder…?"

"Her name was Rei, or so I hear. They found her on the twenty-fifth floor of their headquarters. She tried to escape but made the mistake of leaping out the window. The police even showed up. What a mess. Hmm? Is something wrong?"

"Oh, it's nothing…"

That was, without a doubt, her old tutor. Shiren wasn't sure why she was here, but it was likely she was looking for something.

If it were anyone else, I'd be asking if they survived, but I have a feeling Rei would somehow make it out of a fall from the twenty-fifth floor... Probably.

Once she determined Rei was most likely fine, Shiren stopped thinking.

"Because of that, among other things, the meeting got started a little late. It's fine, though, since the nation's still running smoothly."

"Sounds like you had a busy day. Do you want some tea?"

"You don't need to attend to little things like that. You can be more imposing, Shiren. You're the emperor. There's nothing you need to worry about."

Shiren remained silent, biting her lip. Her worries were only growing. In fact, they were already threatening to crush her. But she couldn't give up now—she still hadn't told Sairi anything.

"Mom? I have a favor to ask."

"What is it? If there's something you want, just ask. Don't hold back. You've done enough of that in your life already."

Sairi's smile was big and kind. It was like an embrace, easily wrapping Shiren up in its warmth.

And yet it wasn't enough.

"I—I want to see everyone I left behind in the Empire..."

Shiren had fully intended to look Sairi in the eyes when she said that, but she found her head drooping instead. She was afraid. What if Sairi didn't understand? Even if she said the words, it would be pointless if she couldn't communicate her real feelings.

"Shiren..."

All that came back was her name. Was Sairi going to be angry with her? Disappointed in her?

"I'm lonely... Mom..."

Shiren felt herself tense up. Waiting for an answer was painful. This was the loneliest she'd been in her entire life.

She might have been able to bear it if she'd never known anything else, but back in the old Empire, Shiren had experienced a life that was, quite frankly, like a dream. She'd come to appreciate happiness.

"Of course."

As she sat there, gaze downcast, she felt a gentle force pressing around her.

Sairi was hugging her.

"I should have noticed sooner. I'm sorry. I don't have a lot of experience as a mother."

"No, it's okay. I should have said something..." Shiren's lips turned up in a smile.

She recalled what Kiyomizu had said: Giving up on something before you needed to was the same as running away. It was careless.

A path was opening up before her, all because she had mustered the courage to step forward.

"You don't have to stay away from them forever, of course," Sairi said as she stroked Shiren's hair. "I don't intend to start a conflict with Akinomiya for decades. I'll see what I can do."

"Really?! How soon?!" Shiren's eyes went wide. So people actually understood her when she expressed her feelings—there had been no need to worry.

"Can you wait a year? That should be enough time for me to figure something out."

"What?"

A whole *year*? That was way too long. She wouldn't make it in time.

Relationships between people were like food: They had expiration dates. Once that date passed, they would fizzle away, like they'd never existed in the first place.

From her reaction, Sairi seemed to understand what was going through Shiren's head.

"Shiren, we've only just created our nation. On the surface, we exist in opposition to the old Empire in Akinomiya. I know it sounds stupid, but adults can't offer their support without little reasons like that. We need help from a lot of people to get a new country off the ground. That's why I worked to show that we're different from the old Empire—so that we can gather that support."

Sairi's words washed over Shiren. Her mother had understood, but it hadn't changed anything. Shiren couldn't move the world of adults with feelings alone.

"So if we go and make up with the old Empire barely a month into our existence, all the people who came to support us will be very upset. Then everything we've worked to build will collapse around us. All we've done now is apply the glue. It'll be another year before it dries and sets. I guess that feels a little long to you, Shiren. You don't experience time the same way adults do, after all."

A *little* long?

"Isn't there anything we can do...?" asked Shiren.

"You went through a difficult time where you were all by yourself, didn't you?"

How could she ever forget?

Ouen had died, Sairi had vanished, and Shiren had been ejected from the castle—she'd spent her days treated like a criminal. Even now, she had no idea how she'd managed to overcome that hardship.

It must have been because she never once consciously thought of "overcoming" it. She had hunkered down and sat still, as though waiting for a storm to pass, and eventually found that it had ended.

She had been like a lifeless zombie, just doing what she could to avoid dying again.

But Shiren was no longer a zombie. Her heart had come back to life because of Ryouta and the others. And that heart wasn't going to last a year.

She would become a zombie and lose all feeling again. She wouldn't even be jealous or envious. Her emotions would simply vanish.

But only Shiren knew that about herself.

"I know it might sound odd coming from me, but you didn't give in back then. You'll be fine. You know exactly how long you need to wait this time, and—hey, you're the emperor now."

Shiren knew what her mother meant. Back then, it would have been impossible to believe she could be treated this well. She was more than blessed in the material sense. So much so, she was probably due for some karmic punishment. People no longer looked at her with distaste—instead, they had worship in their eyes.

The problem was that wasn't enough to fill the hole in her heart.

She didn't need material wealth. She didn't need reputation.

I wonder what Ryouta's doing right now...

Her days with Ryouta had been so much fun. This lifeless hotel room stood no chance against them.

She could remember being frustrated with him, getting angry, and worrying over him, but looking back, she found she now cherished all of it. Not even she understood why. She began to wonder if Ryouta had been exuding some kind of intoxicating cloud.

He must be having a great time with Big Sis, though...

If she could, she wanted to put everything back the way it was and stay by Ryouta's side. She knew that would never happen, though. It would be asking way too much. Everyone would probably be disappointed with her if she so much as said it out loud.

But either way, she at least wanted to go back.

"I'm the emperor, right, Mom?" Shiren asked. Her tone and expression were calm, like a child asking for her mother's permission.

"Of course. If you weren't, we'd have a huge problem on our hands." Sairi offered a relieved smile—maybe she had sensed an Imperial dignity in Shiren's bearing.

The emperor was the most powerful person in this country. That meant she didn't have to listen to the archbishop.

Shiren had found her answer.

And so she decided it was time to start her rebellious phase.

The next day, Sairi returned home late again.

Shiren would normally have been lonely, but this time, it was a stroke of luck.

She took the note out from the drawer.

This is the first decision I've made since leaving the Sacred Blood Empire.

Her hands were shaking. Slowly, she punched the number into the phone. Each press had a terrible weight to it, as though she was inputting the code for a missile launch. Perhaps history itself would change because of her selfishness, if only a little.

Once she'd pressed the last number, the line connected.

"Hello, this is the Holy Sacred Blood Empire PR Department—"

If Kiyomizu could be trusted, Shiren just had to vent to whoever was at the end of this line.

But what if she was wrong? What if a random person from the Holy Sacred Blood Empire answered?

Even if there was an informant or a mole somewhere in the organization, that didn't necessarily mean they would answer the phone.

She might be making a fatal mistake.

M-maybe this isn't a good idea... I have no way to check, though...

"—This is customer-service representative Kiyomizu Jouryuuji!"

"Hey, why are you answering the phones?!" All of Shiren's apprehensions vanished as she made the jab at Kiyomizu. "Whose side are you on?! Are you everywhere at once?!"

"Why must I suffer the indignity of working under the people who usurped the order of the Virginal Father? My family's finances may be in shambles, but about one and a half billion of my own assets were left untouched. From that, I withdrew about three hundred million and bought a few people off."

"You have *that* much money?! I never imagined you had it *that* good in life!"

"Money can't buy happiness."

"That sounds a little hypocritical coming from a billionaire!"

"More importantly, you understand what it means for you to call me, right?"

"Oh, uh, yeah..."

All of Shiren's tension had vanished the moment she heard a familiar voice.

"If you have no need of me, then I'm hanging up. You know I'm not obligated to help you, right?"

"I—I want to go back..."

"If you don't finish your sentence, I can't tell where you want to go."

"I want to go back to the Sacred Blood Empire. I want to be with my friends..."

At Kiyomizu's urging, Shiren was finally able to put her feelings into words.

There was a short delay before Kiyomizu gave her response.

"Well said. I see you've progressed."

"M-maybe..."

"Then all you need to do is cross the border. It's so close! Only a little over nine kilometers away as the crow flies."

"I can't. The entire hotel is surrounded by people from the new order..."

Sairi's underlings were positioned so as not to give them any blind spots—not even an ant could slip through unnoticed.

At a glance, they appeared to be hotel security, but they were, in fact, members of the order of the Virginal Father. These were not members of the Kiyomizu family's faction, but those under Sairi's control.

Of course, they were there to protect Shiren, not to keep her locked up. But right now, there was little difference between the two.

"That level of security is nothing. I came in through the window last time, remember?"

"Don't act like I'm the same as you! That was totally a humblebrag!"

"In that case, I'll see what I can do to create a favorable scenario."

"A favorable scenario?"

"Yes. You'll still have to do your part, though."

Shiren finally had her chance. A smile crossed her face for the first time in a while.

"All right, I'll make sure I succeed!"

"Oh, I forgot to mention one thing."

"Hm? What is it?"

"Just because you've told me how you feel over the phone, that doesn't make everything okay. There's someone else you need to make sure to tell."

"Huh...?"

"Well, no one asks a go-between to propose marriage. Anyway, I'll be calling to follow up."

Kiyomizu abruptly hung up, cutting Shiren off.

"She's really not the nurturing type, huh..."

Shiren sighed and turned to look out the window. As usual, the city was glimmering in the dark.

Shiren, too, thought the night view was beautiful. For some reason, it seemed to be asking her to stay—that a passing moment of hesitation would make a mess of the rest of her life.

"No, I am going...to..."

Her voice was weak. She had told Kiyomizu, but would she be able to say it again to someone else?

"I need to tell...Ryouta...and my sister..."

Shiren saw her face reflected in the mirror in front of the desk. Her expression was just as apprehensive as it had been before she made the phone call.

There were still many hurdles to overcome.

Scritch, scratch, scritch.

Ryouta could hear the sound of pen on paper from his side.

Scratch, scritch, scratch.

He needed to do his homework, too, but the sound was so loud in his ears that he couldn't concentrate.

Scritch, scratch, scritch. Scratch, scritch, scratch. Scritch, scratch, scritch.

"Hey... Ouka?"

Unable to put up with the noise anymore, Ryouta spoke up with a frown.

"What? I'm not showing you my answers. You can do this on your own," Ouka replied, her expression blank. She seemed fully focused.

"That's not what I meant. Shouldn't we do this in different rooms...? I can't relax."

"Why? You're my minion—stay by my side."

"That's true, but we don't have to do our homework right next to each other..."

"This is what the work of a minion entails. Do your job."

The work of a minion. When she put it that way, there was really nothing he could say back.

"My minions need to have a relatively high level of academic ability. Get into a good college. Get in through the back door if you must."

"Why are you already considering illegal options?!"

"Incidentally, you can legally be accepted at the University of the Sacred Blood Empire even if your grades are bad, so long as you pay twenty times normal tuition."

"Stop trying to legitimize shady deals!"

"If you don't want to pay, then study."

It isn't that I don't want to study. It's just kind of difficult in this situation...

It wasn't that he hated being around Ouka. Not at all. In fact, getting to study in the same room as his first crush was one of the greatest privileges of his life.

But something's different...

If they were still in love with each other, shouldn't they have a different sort of relationship?

To put it frankly, shouldn't they be boyfriend and girlfriend?

That seemed like the normal order of things, but it didn't seem like they were heading in that direction.

They were just existing in the same apartment together. It felt more like he was living with a grouchy sister.

Ryouta's actual sister, Rei, had doted on him because of his curse, so he'd never actually had the experience of living with a grouchy sister. If he had, though, she'd probably have been like Ouka.

Am I supposed to ask her out...? Hmm... But she did explicitly call me her minion earlier...

He had a feeling the "minion" excuse was turning every relationship here into something lukewarm and noncommittal.

Sure—it was effective when two people weren't close. Serving as someone's minion was a much more intimate relationship than being strangers. But once that distance had been closed, things were a little different. If they tried to get closer, the status of "minion" would push them back apart, like two magnets with the same polarity.

I never wanted to be her minion. I wanted to be her boyfriend.

"You haven't touched your homework for some time now." Ouka was staring at him.

"W-we all work at our own pace, okay...? Are *you* done?"

"Yes. I finished a while ago. You know I've received special lessons for gifted students since I was a child."

Ouka attended school and did her homework, but it seemed that was only a formality.

"Special lessons? Did Shiren have to take those, too…?"

"She dropped out after ten minutes on the first day and never attended another session."

"That's way too early to drop out!"

"I remember our tutor saying, 'She must have been born under an unlucky star.'"

"It was so bad that they had to bring fate into it?!"

"*Sigh*, and now we're talking about Shiren." Ouka planted her elbows on the table and rested her head in her folded hands.

"Oh… Sorry…"

"Why are you apologizing? It's not as though I'm trying to forget her. I never could."

Ouka flipped through her notebook, as though stalling for time. Ryouta could feel a little gust from the movement of the pages.

"Just a moment ago, you were wondering if we should move things forward, weren't you, Ryouta? If this is really all there is to living together."

"Basically, yeah."

"I don't want things to stay like this, either. I want us to be all over each other."

"'All over each other'…?"

"Oh, don't get blushy about it. That's what happens when you live together. But I can't stop thinking about Shiren, and I just can't get in the mood because of it. I guess I'm a lot nicer than I thought."

They were supposed to be moving on with their relationship, but the past—Shiren, that is—was holding them back.

"I feel the same way. And Alfoncina, when she called me to the roof earlier—she was really mad at me."

Maybe she couldn't stand to see Ryouta walking around like a shadow of his former self. As someone older than him, she could probably see all his faults.

"Hmph. She has no right to be angry with you. She is just like me." Ouka's mood turned sour as soon as she heard Alfoncina's name.

"What do you mean by that? Oh, because both of you hold power and you're both schemers?"

"There's no point in hiding it anymore, so I'll just tell you. She has a crush on you, Ryouta."

"Uh-huh, okay........................ Wait, what?!" Ryouta dropped his pencil. He couldn't even think about studying at this point.

"Keep your voice down. I'm honestly shocked that *you're* shocked after all this time."

"But why would she have a crush on *me*? There are way better people out there…"

"Romantic relations cannot form between two people who have never met and don't know each other. That's all there is to it. People of high status have very few chances to meet those of the opposite sex, which makes it easy for misunderstandings to occur. That is all."

Ouka apparently had no qualms about sharing Alfoncina's feelings freely.

"Should you have told me this…?" Ryouta, on the other hand, was feeling a little guilty.

"It won't change anything. Alfoncina knows her station. She will not cross any lines, and I know *you* aren't going to ask her out. See? No problem."

"You're pretty ruthless, even to your elders…"

"I'd prefer it if you saw this as an expression of my close, casual relationship with her. She's an adult, after all. She'll be fine. The problem is…the child."

"You mean Shiren…?" He couldn't think of anyone else.

Ouka didn't give a verbal reply, but the discontent and discomfort in her eyes was confirmation enough.

"*Sigh*. If only your parting with Shiren had been more of a clear break."

"I wish I could put an end to her," Ouka muttered.

"Whoa, don't put it like that…"

That almost sounded like she wanted to kill her sister.

"I used that word on purpose. If we don't put an end to her, we'll be stuck like this forever. Meanwhile, she's having a grand old time in that new Empire of hers. It's not fair."

"I guess… But it's not like we can just wander over and say hi. We haven't even established diplomatic relations yet."

"Exactly. We can't reach out first, or we'd lose face. That would mean we'd acknowledged their existence as a nation."

Obviously, they couldn't acknowledge an entity that would go on to oppose them.

"Yeah…"

Shiren's departure from the Empire wasn't just a personal affair. She now stood at the top of a very troubling organization. Ouka's position essentially prevented her from reaching out.

It would be difficult even to create a point of contact. Physically, the distance wasn't very great, and yet Shiren felt so far away.

"But that was the better thing to do at the time."

Ouka's gaze dropped to her worksheet. Her answers were written in handwriting so neat that they could have been printed on the page. Ryouta didn't know the correct answers himself, but he was pretty sure she had gotten them all right. He didn't even see any eraser marks. There were no traces of doubt.

Ryouta followed her gaze and wished the answer to their own problems was as clear-cut.

Better did not mean ideal. When Shiren had announced she would be leaving, she was clearly unhappy. Did they have no choice but to continue their lives on parallel tracks like this, never meeting again?

Just then, Ouka's phone rang.

"Hello, what is it? Let me guess—the bill raising taxes we were keeping secret from the public was leaked by the tabloids? You'll have to stop publication. Now."

It sounded like Ouka was up to no good again.

"What…? When did that…?"

She was now fully concentrated on her phone call.

Whatever the news was, it came as a shock. Ouka's eyes were open so wide, they looked like they'd fall out of her skull. Ryouta watched her, hoping it wasn't anything bad. It sounded like she was being fed a rather lengthy explanation.

"Of course. There's no problem if they're the ones approaching us. But this sounds a little fishy. Would Sairi really do something that doesn't benefit them at all?"

Ryouta could only hear Ouka's side of the conversation, but he could tell this was something vital to the country.

"Well, even if it *is* a trap, we just need to be prepared, and we won't fall for it."

There was confidence in her eyes.

"Fine, I give my consent. At least it will clear this proverbial fog, though I'm not sure what will happen when the sun's finally out. I don't think anyone does. All right, move things along, but quietly. Put a hold on the five-year tax-increase project."

"Was that about the Holy Sacred Blood Empire...?"

"Yes. It sounds as though their leader wants to meet with us. She wants to discuss the future of the Sacred Blooded."

"Does that mean Shiren is—?"

"Yes." There was a complex mix of emotions on Ouka's face. "I don't know what she's thinking, but this might be my chance to put an end to her."

"Please don't take things too far..."

"I don't plan to. But even I have no idea how things are going to pan out. At least, I won't until we see her. This whole thing is a black box."

Ryouta understood what she meant. "I haven't figured out my own feelings yet, either. I'm happy I'll be able to see her, but I'm also terrified. But either way, I have to go."

All paths were converging on a single point. Every one of them would have to experience this event or remain unable to grow and mature.

"Yes. This will serve as a rite of passage, a step toward the next stage of our lives. Of course, there's always a chance we won't succeed."

Then a wistful smile spread across Ouka's face.

"*Sigh-*. This must be how Shiren felt, right before she reunited with Sairi."

"What is the meaning of this?! No one told me anything!"

Sairi was hounding the PR department.

An outrageous decision had been made without her knowledge. Some-one had asked the leader of the Sacred Blood Empire for the opportunity to meet, and they had done so in the name of the leader of the Holy Sacred Blood Empire.

This was premature. *Far* too premature. There were quite a few obsta-cles left to overcome before they could even start thinking of mutual concessions.

"My deepest apologies… Her Majesty stated that you were already aware of this, Lady Sairi…"

The manager of the PR department was in disbelief as she bowed her head over and over. She, too, had been shocked that diplomacy was pro-ceeding without Sairi's knowledge. This whole affair was a bolt from the blue.

But it was already too late.

Their side had just asked for a meeting. They couldn't just call back and say, *Sorry, we changed our minds.*

What I don't understand is why no one brought this up with me… I'm almost certain there are no factions or cliques in my organization… Could there be a traitor from Akinomiya in our ranks? But I thought I'd conducted thorough background checks of all employees…

No—perhaps she was thinking about this too hard.

Sairi considered the matter once again.

This was Shiren's decision.

She remembered how pained Shiren had looked when she'd told her to wait a year.

If Shiren really did make this decision on her own, then that wouldn't neces-sarily be a bad thing. That would mean she's trying to carve her own path.

Sairi's expression softened.

Now that she thought about it, she realized Shiren had never been the type to make big decisions like this. Even when she spoke like an adult, she hesitated to set her own direction—she was the type to fall behind and let others lead. It probably didn't help that her older sister was the type to act boldly in front of a crowd, but either way, Shiren had been stuck in the role of little sister.

That hadn't been a problem in the past. Ouka was destined to lead a country in the future, and all that was asked of Shiren was to behave and stay out of her sister's way.

But now that Shiren was emperor of the Holy Sacred Blood Empire, that wasn't enough.

It was a good thing if she'd done some growing up while Sairi wasn't looking. No one was going to die as a result of this decision.

"What's on the docket for the meeting anyway?"

A smile back on her face, Sairi resumed gathering information.

"U-um… Well, it will be a social gathering over a meal and will take place at the restaurant on the top floor of the Oshiro Royal Hotel."

The bewildered PR manager told Sairi everything she knew.

"Hmm, I doubt there will be much political talk in a situation like that. All right. I'll readjust the schedule for that day. We'll manage somehow. I'll take charge of the menu, too. We'll give them the warmest welcome imaginable."

Sairi's anger melted away, and the PR manager seemed genuinely relieved.

That was when Shiren came in.

"Mom…"

She looked like a guilty child whose pranks had been found out. Sairi knew that expression—Shiren was aware she'd done something bad.

She's had that same expression ever since she was a child. Well, she is still a child, after all.

It warmed her heart, and she felt the urge to scold Shiren melt away. This girl couldn't pull off a complicated scheme even if she wanted to.

"I'm sorry! I wanted to see everyone so badly, and…" She ducked her head timidly. "…I couldn't help it. I acted on my own, and—"

"I heard what happened. To be honest, this wasn't a good move, but it's already been scheduled, so we're going forward with it. I'll make sure the schedules of all those meant to attend will be open."

Sairi smiled and patted her daughter's head.

That's right. I have no right to scold her.

There'd been no way to take Shiren when she fled, but whatever her reasons, Sairi had still left her behind. No excuse would ever be good enough. For that reason, she would accept little things like this.

If Shiren caused problems for someone else, then it was Sairi's own fault—she was the one who had raised her, after all.

It wasn't like Shiren was going anywhere.

"It's natural to want to see your friends. There's nothing to be embarrassed about."

"Th-thanks...Mom..."

"You must have wanted to do this so much that you didn't care if I scolded you, right? And that means there's no point in me getting angry with you. Just make us proud as the emperor of our new empire."

"Yeah. Okay. I'll do my best..."

As Sairi patted her head, a mixed expression crossed Shiren's face.

Sairi didn't notice that expression. Nor did she notice that, unbeknownst to her, her daughter was becoming someone new—someone she couldn't control.

Meanwhile, Shiren knew that Sairi no longer understood her. She had changed so drastically in such a short amount of time, after all. She had gone through things her mother could never imagine.

If she wanted to outwit Sairi, she would have to use that to her advantage.

Her chances of success were slim. No—not even Shiren knew how things would turn out or even what she really wanted.

But she had to do it.

She would be giving up on so many things if she quit now.

The feelings in the depths of her heart were telling her she *had* to see them.

"I'm sorry, Mom," she said, barely a whisper, not loud enough for Sairi to hear.

"Hmm? Did you say something?"

"No, nothing."

Characters

Ominaeshi Sarano

Ouka's mother. Fought over Ouka's father, Ouen, with his mistress, Sairi. Lives in the castle basement pursuing her nerdy hobbies and unique aesthetic tastes.

Sairi Fuyukura

Shiren's mother. The woman who took over the order of the Virginal Father and founded the Holy Sacred Blood Empire in Oshiro. Descendant of Progenitor Alfoncina.

EPISODE 3
LET'S ALL GO TO THE NEW EMPIRE!

The charter bus taking Ryouta and the others out of the Sacred Blood Empire slowly crossed the border and into the city of Oshiro.

"Once we get through the mountain pass, it's a straight shot to central Oshiro," Ouka murmured to herself as she sat by the window, watching the scenery go by. The bus moved at a slow and safe pace through the cedar trees. Ryouta sat beside her, staring at his hands in his lap.

"I wonder how Shiren's doing..."

It had been only a month since Shiren left. But in the meantime, things had started to change. He had a feeling that, if they didn't see her *now*, she would transform into someone completely different.

When he saw her on TV now, she seemed more mature than she had in those first few days. It seemed like she'd finally accepted her role as emperor.

"Why the long face, Ryouta? We're going for dinner! What's wrong?"

A cheerful voice called out from the seat behind his—it was Alfoncina.

She leaned over into his and Ouka's space. She was cooling herself with a paper fan that was apparently *YouRou IKou!* merchandise; it was covered in familiar characters.

"Alfoncina? You seem like a different person compared with the last time I saw you..."

He remembered how serious she'd looked when they'd met on the rooftop.

"I said everything I needed to say. All that's left is see how things turn out."

"I guess so..."

Ryouta, for his part, had no plans beyond meeting Shiren.

"None of us know how this dinner will turn out~. Though we've set things up so every scenario will be favorable to us. Isn't that right, Ouka?" Alfoncina asked, hiding the curl of her grin behind her fan.

"I suppose so. I know what I need to come out victorious, at any rate."

"Oh? And what's that?"

"Once we see that Shiren's enjoying life in her new country, we'll all live happily ever after."

Both Alfoncina and Ryouta knew exactly what that meant. If Shiren was happy, then Ouka didn't need to worry about her anymore.

That would mean she could think about Ryouta all day without feeling guilty. And the same went for Ryouta, of course.

"If that doesn't seem to be the case, then what will you do?" Alfoncina asked, a mischievous smile crossing her face.

"There's no need to think about things that won't happen, **Kimmers**."

"P-please don't give me awful nicknames based on my real name! Besides, that doesn't sound like an appropriate way to refer to a beautiful woman like me!"

"Wow, that was effective. I'll be sure to tuck that away for the next time I'm angry with you."

"Please! Anything but that!"

"Shut up, Kimmiserable."

"*Gasp*, you modified it! At this point, I'd rather you used my real name!"

"You should be proud of your real name, Mattie."

"You're making me sound like an old fishing buddy! Like you'd run into me on the street and say, *Hey, Mattie! Let's grab a pint at the pub later!*"

"We're on the bus now, Mattie, please keep your voice down. Don't you have some squid to munch on, Kimmers?"

"Please stop making up a personality for me! I don't have any squid! And please don't use two nicknames in one sentence!"

At some point in the conversation, the mood had gone right back to normal.

"Argh, enough! This whole thing is a mess; let's clear the air with some karaoke! Bus guide! Can you get out the mic?"

"I'm eating chips right now, so can you wait?" said Kokoko. "*Munch, munch, munch.*"

"Hey! Why is Kokoko our bus guide?!" asked Ryouta.

She was even wearing a bus-guide uniform. It was too big for her, though, so it was loose in places.

"Oh, I chose her for the job to save on costs. She was invited, too."

"Of *course* it's to cut costs…"

"Now, if you look out to your right, you'll see a cedar tree," Kokoko began. "And if you look to your left, you'll see a cedar tree. This is a forest. We are on a mountain. We can see dirt. There's a rock."

"Bus guide, please, that's not necessary! We can see that all ourselves!"

"And here, we have a fox." Kokoko pointed at herself, even though she had rabbit ears on top of her head.

"This has to be a joke, right? You're not still insisting you're a fox, are you?"

"How dare you ridicule me, human," she spat back in the haughty tone of a god. "Now, please take another look out your window. There's a cedar. I'd say it rivals the likes of the Tokyo Skytree."

"*How*, though?! What about it makes you say that?!"

"And I'd say the mountains around here are about one-eighth the size of the Tokyo Dome."

"I'm asking *why* you're saying that, though! And one-eighth isn't even very big!"

"Here's an interesting piece of trivia: Cedars produce pollen."

"We know that! Most people know that!"

"Here's another interesting piece of trivia: The first bus guides in Japan worked for the Kamenoi Bus company in Oita Prefecture in the mid-twentieth century. They were employed on the Beppu hot-springs circuit. Now there are many more small bus companies than there used to be, quite a few of which don't have guides."

"Why do you know so much about that one specific topic?!"

"All right, here is your microphone. Sing whatever you want, however you want."

Kokoko handed Alfoncina the microphone, the remote control, and the songbook.

"All right~. I think I'll go with this one today~."

Akinomiya Traveling

Oh, tell me you love me, even if you don't mean it
Keep me from the cold wind
I'll turn a blind eye to your infidelity
Since I don't have what it takes to win your affections

Ahh, the nights in Akinomiya are so much colder than
Oshiro
The last train comes in at twelve thirty
My body's cold, hold me just for tonight
Oh, oh, Akinomiya love ♪

"Why are you singing *enka* like an old person?!"

"Nice one, Mattie! Excellent tremolo! You're the Imperial Songstress!"

"Stop calling me Mattie!"

"Then don't sing songs that make people want to call you Mattie, Alfoncina! Sing something a little more modern!"

That song had been much more suited to the name *Matsuko Kimura* than the name *Alfoncina*.

"She can't, Ryouta. This karaoke machine is pretty old. It doesn't have any new songs. It only has songs up to the early nineties."

"So we can only sing golden oldies?!"

"It's fine. The only kind of people who sing karaoke on a bus anymore are old people."

"Hey! Ouka! You know I'm still in high school, right?!" Alfoncina protested.

"That's pretty weak coming from someone who just sang *enka*."

"Everyone has their own interests. As I've said before, my real job is drawing manga, but I do archbishop work on the side as a hobby!"

"Being an archbishop is supposed to be your job!" Ryouta exclaimed. "It's not something you can do as a hobby!"

Alfoncina's comment was very unbecoming of an archbishop.

"It's all right, Ryouta," Ouka said. "Imperial law states that minors are not allowed to work as full-time employees, so legally, both her manga and archbishop work would be classed as hobbies."

"You can't explain the problem away with legal technicalities! This is about her intent!"

"Yes! I intend to keep working hard every day so I can be an even better manga artist. I hope to take *YouRou IKou!* to very interesting places."

"I wasn't talking about your manga! I was talking about dedication to your work as an archbishop!"

"Lately, I've seen a lot more offerings and votive tablets at shrines featuring fanart of *YouRo IKou!*, so I made a place specifically for people to hang those up."

"That's where you're focusing your efforts?!"

They really just do whatever they want in this country, Ryouta thought.

"I think New Progenitor Alfoncina might be taking believers away from you at this rate..."

"Ryouta, the most important thing is not the number of followers I have. I don't mind if she takes some away from me."

"You probably should mind." Ryouta wished she would take her job a little more seriously.

"Don't worry about that, Ryouta. According to our constitution, every citizen of the Sacred Blood Empire is a member of the Holy Church of the Sacred Blood, so statistically, the number of believers is equal to our population and is unlikely to go down."

"I don't care if you're manipulating the numbers!"

"Ryouta, that's absurd. If belief was all it took to maintain a religious organization, things would be easy. The one who stands at the top doesn't just need to know how to lead—they need to be able to keep the organization running smoothly, too. Honestly, the ability to lead is pretty irrelevant. Organizational skills are much more important."

"*Your* opinions are absurd! You can't just go around saying things like that!"

"But the father of management, Drucker, said so himself!"

"No, he didn't! I haven't read up on him, but I'm sure he never said that!"

Ouka rummaged around in her things and pulled out a book. Ryouta spotted the word *Management* on the cover. It must be one of Drucker's works.

"As the emperor, I have read through this book. I thought I might find hints about how to manipulate the public."

"Couldn't you have picked a more wholesome reason?!"

"Oh, wait. The quote I just recited wasn't Drucker; it was Truccer."

"This Truccer person sounds like a fraud!"

"The author's history is right here. Want to check it out?"

> Truccer
> I chose this pen name because I happened to be watching a TV show about long-haul truckers. During the day, I work full-time at a company, and at night, I publish books on admin and management. Notable works include *Administration from the Perspective of Professional Baseball Player Quotes*, *Management Lessons from Famous Sportsmen*, *Companies That Could Work in Theory*, *150 Start-Up Trivia Facts*, *Admin Turnarounds à la Sun Tzu*, and more. Real name: Matsutarou Kimura.

"This guy can't be serious... He can't really be taking quotes from baseball players and using them to run a business... And he's treating it with the same reverence as the one using life lessons from a Warring States–period general..." Ryouta held his head in his hands. "And there's nothing more suspicious than the fact that he's using a pen name... Actually, isn't this name...?"

"Matsutarou Kimura is my father..."

Alfoncina had raised her hand, obviously wishing they could have steered clear of this subject. Her eyes looked hollow.

"I knew it! I thought it sounded familiar!"

"He likes *enka*."

"So it runs in the family! And he even published a book referencing Sun Tzu. Is that…?"

"When I saw it, I knew *YouRou IKou!* could work… This is so embarrassing; please don't make me say any more…" Alfoncina hid her face behind her fan.

For some reason, the group at the front of the bus was getting louder and more excited.

At the same time, a great wave of negative energy was starting to waft forward from the back of the bus.

"Oh, this feels like…"

Ryouta sat up in his seat and saw Tamaki way in the back, her face pale.

"Ooh… I don't feel well… And right when I get invited to a state dinner, even though I am a miserable little peasant who could never hope to influence political affairs… I have no excuse… Where's my sick bag? Where's my sick bag…?"

"Shijou, are you okay? You don't look so good… I guess these small mountain roads kind of make you dizzy, huh?"

The Sacred Blood Empire sat in a valley, so they had to pass through the mountains in order to reach Oshiro by car.

Back when Akinomiya belonged to Japan, there was a highway that ran through the city, leading to a long tunnel through the mountain. But that had been completely closed off and was now off-limits.

"I would have brought some medicine for my stomach if I knew this was going to happen…"

Tamaki's response came as a bit of a surprise to Ryouta.

"Stomach medicine? Shouldn't you have brought motion-sickness medicine instead?"

Her face wasn't just pale—it was purple. Her hands were shaking, too.

"Did you eat something bad?"

"This…"

With a shaky hand, she pointed to a big bag. It was stuffed full of jam rolls.

"I couldn't just throw away the hundred thousand jam rolls I accidentally ordered, so that's all I've been eating, and now I feel sick…"

"You've just overeaten, then!"

"That, and it's almost ten days past the expiration date, which probably didn't help... Not all of them could fit in the fridge... Though, I guess someone like me deserves to eat expired pastries..."

"You don't need to sacrifice yourself like that! You don't need to digest any of that food—just throw it up!"

Ryouta started slowly rubbing Tamaki's back. She was hunched over from nausea.

"Oh... Ryouta, don't bother... I can both vomit and die by myself..."

"You don't have to die! Get rid of that old food!"

There was still some distance between them and their destination, so it would be much better for her to just throw it up. Ryouta continued to gently rub her back.

"N-no, it's okay... You have Her Imperial Majesty, so..."

"Huh? Why are you bringing up Ouka...?" Tamaki's face went from purple to red. That wasn't a normal symptom of car sickness. "I feel like I might get the wrong idea again if you keep stroking me like this... I'll develop weird feelings, even though I know I should give up..."

"About what?" Ryouta was finding this hard to follow.

"Oh, I suppose even if I tell you now, you two are already a thing... Should I...?"

"Do you have some kind of deep, dark secret or something...?"

"Yes... I think I can muster a little courage and try again...that is, if I ever get the chance, of course. Though, I feel like I may find myself at the bottom of a ravine instead."

"Can you not say things like that when we're on a bus?!"

That was the last thing Ryouta wanted to hear as they drove up a mountain road.

Just then, Bus Guide Kokoko approached.

"You've grown up, Big Sis Tamaki. Tell 'im how you feel. Go for the killing blow."

"Did we really need more violence in this conversation?"

"That's what her world is like, though. Not that you'd ever understand."

For some reason, Kokoko was acting like a mother watching over her child. She stood with her arms crossed, a proud look on her face.

Though, I guess in terms of age, she's more like an ancestor than a mom...

Tamaki stared hard at Ryouta. It was like she was trying to communicate with him through means other than speech.

"Okay, I'm going to say it… Ryouta, for a very long time, I've—"

More and more emotion bubbled up into her words.

Then something else bubbled up, too—from her stomach.

"…Bl-bleeech! Hurk! Urk!"

She threw up.

"You okay, Shijou? That was kind of impressive, honestly…"

"Ah-ha, ha-ha-ha, ha-ha-ha… Ha-ha…"

Her eyes turned hollow, but there was still half of a smile on her face. It was a rather frightening expression.

"Ha-ha… This is just how it goes for me… Do people usually vomit with such perfect timing…? That was enough to kill even everlasting love. Please laugh at me. Spit at me, even. I'm sure it would be much cleaner than whatever comes out of my mouth… You could use your spit to disinfect me… Ha-ha…"

"Big Sis Tamaki, let me say this to you as a god's daughter: You should probably get either blessed or exorcised. You can believe in things like that. I think you're reaching a limit. Not even someone like me could've predicted this." Kokoko seemed shocked. "Just rinse your mouth out for now, okay? Think of it as a purification ceremony."

"This is who I am, Kokoko… Ha-ha…"

"Um, Shijou? Let's get this wiped down…," said Ryouta. "I'll grab some tissues…"

Even he was a little shocked after such a grim sight.

"O-okay… I'm sorry you have to do all that for filth like me—I'm not better than vomit… I feel so bad for the tissues that must absorb it… Ah-ha-ha-ha-ha…"

"Big Sis Tamaki, I know this isn't the best way to put it, but you look like you've just been sexually assaulted… Sorry… I would have stopped you if I had known this would happen…"

Ouka shouted from the front, "Hey! It smells like yogurt in here!" Which was just rubbing salt in the wound.

"Be a little more considerate, Ouka…," Ryouta complained as he started to clean up. He used tissues to wipe up the mess, collected them in a plastic bag, then threw it away in one of the garbage cans.

"I'm sorry, Ryouta... My head is blank, and I don't think I'll be able to move for a while..."

Tamaki sat in the aisle, leaning against a nearby seat.

"It's fine, it's fine. Look at it this way—it'd be completely awful for this to happen at school right in front of your crush, right? Here, though, it's just embarrassing, and— Hey, Shijou, why are you crying?"

Tamaki wasn't just crying; she was bawling. Even her faint smile had vanished.

"You struck the killing blow so smoothly, Ryouta... You're awful. Really awful. Not even the cruelest god would do this to her..."

Kokoko had moved right past criticism and to absolute disgust with him. Her ears were drooping even more than normal.

"Kokoko," Tamaki spoke up. "I've put my feelings into words. Will you listen?"

"Oh, sure..."

My life is a sea of a billion regrets, and I am drowning.
Tamaki Shijou

This was far too dark. Both Ryouta and Kokoko had no idea what to say. *I feel like* That's nice *isn't going to cut it here...*

"Big Sis Tamaki... I made a vow to do everything in my power until you're happy...," Kokoko said with utter sincerity, gripping Tamaki's hand. "And I will, no matter how much suffering I must inflict on others..."

That sounds kind of ominous...

*The bus stopped briefly so Tamaki could rinse out her mouth.

"*Phew*, this has been an eventful ride..." The bus was getting ready to take off again, so Ryouta returned to his own seat.

"Indeed," came a voice from the aisle. "I was sitting nearby, so I witnessed Shijou and her determination."

It was Sasara, on her way back to her seat in the rear. She still hadn't totally recovered, so she was using a cane.

"Is that what that was…? Oh yeah, I never got to hear what she had to say…"

Whatever it was had eventually been obscured by her incident.

"You are truly thickheaded. But I suppose none of us would want you to grow too sharp, so— Urgh—"

She seemed pained as she walked—her wounds were still hurting her.

Her face twisted unconsciously. She had taken the brunt of Sairi's full power, unlike Ryouta, so her recovery was going much slower.

"Hey, I'll lend you my shoulder. Hang on to me."

"I can make it on my own…"

"But you were injured because of me."

Ryouta's eyes were earnest, and Sasara grimaced.

"I wish you would let me forget, but it doesn't seem that will be happening… You put Shijou through a lot of pain, too…"

"What are you talking about?"

"Just speaking to myself." Sasara's smile took on a hint of glee. "But if you insist, then I will take you up on the offer. I suppose I'll be much lighter now without my armor on."

Ryouta took Sasara's arm and slung it over his shoulders. "Ah, yes. This should do— Oh."

"Is something the matter?" Sasara asked.

"No, it's nothing. Let's go."

Her chest was pressed right up against him, but he couldn't act weird about it now. He would hate for her to think that he'd volunteered for that reason.

Stay calm, stay calm… I have Ouka…

"You move awkwardly, like a robot… Am I really that heavy…?"

"Not at all. You're light. Super light! Light as a, uh…a sick bag!"

"What a terrible example!" Sasara complained. He'd expected that. But he couldn't help it, considering the timing.

"Sorry! You're not heavy, okay?"

They slowly made their way toward the back.

"Oh, could it be…?" Sasara realized something. "Is it because my chest is touching you?"

Bull's-eye.

"Ha-ha-ha, of course no—"

"You know I can feel it as well, right?" she said coolly.

"Sorry… I wasn't secretly hoping this would happen… I mean it…"

"I know, I know… I do not doubt you, okay?"

Ryouta could tell from her tone that she wasn't angry, but he was still embarrassed.

"I'll try not to let them touch me…"

He was unnecessarily conscious of where her breasts were and had started sweating, but Sasara did eventually get to her seat.

"*Phew.* That was only a few meters, but it felt like two or three times that."

"W-well, why don't you sit down here and rest first before going back, then?"

"Sure, why not?"

The bus had just started moving again. They'd already crossed over into Japan, but they were still in the mountains, so it didn't feel much different. They were winding down a mountain road completely surrounded by cedar trees, just as Kokoko had pointed out.

"I've been listening to all your conversations, by the way."

"I mean, this bus is pretty small, so that was probably inevitable."

Ryouta glanced at Sasara out of the corner of his eye. She was leaning back in her seat, relaxed.

"As I listened, I kept thinking how much of a fool you are."

"Yeah, I know…"

"But you haven't changed a bit. And that was a relief."

"Huh…?"

There was a gentle smile on Sasara's face.

"I figured everything would change drastically after Shiren Fuyukura left. But it really hasn't, and things between all of us are already going back to how they were before. People are frighteningly adaptable."

"Yeah, that day was hell. But we're already moving on, aren't we?"

That was the first time in his life he'd felt such regret and frustration.

Shiren had left, right before Ryouta's eyes. And he was the cause—his own incompetence and powerlessness. If only he'd been strong enough to send Sairi Fuyukura packing, then maybe Shiren would still be with him right now.

That said, he wasn't sure keeping her mother away from her was the right choice, either. Maybe being with Sairi was always what would've made Shiren happiest. The meeting they were headed to was basically a means to confirm whether that was true.

It's so hard to know what's right. *If only right and wrong were as clear in real life as they are in kids' cartoons. Or maybe cartoons are the same, since the villains always think they're doing the right thing.*

"If anything's different," said Sasara, "I suppose it's just that there are fewer people on the bus."

Driver aside, the only passengers were Ryouta, Ouka, Alfoncina, Tamaki, Kokoko, and Sasara. They had additional cars escorting them ahead of and behind the bus, but no guests were riding in those.

There were only six of them.

"Oh yeah, Kiyomizu's gone, too. I guess it can't be helped, though, after what happened to the order."

Apparently, Kiyomizu had been putting up a solitary struggle against Sairi's faction ever since the latter usurped control of the order of the Virginal Father. She was now serving as leader of the resistance.

Ryouta explained all this to Sasara.

"You know quite a lot of detail about this matter. That alone concerns me."

"I mean, she texts me *all the time*..."

He showed Sasara his phone. A line of messages with Kiyomizu's name filled his inbox.

"Wow, that's...quite a lot..."

"She stopped sending me so many texts once she came to the Empire, but now she's started up again... She keeps giving me inside info I'm pretty sure shouldn't be leaked. I might even know more than most of the lower-ranking order members..."

A tired look came over Ryouta's face. He was sometimes overtaken by the urge to delete all her messages and block her, but some of them had important information in them, so he couldn't. And he had a feeling she would just start texting him from a different number anyway.

He checked her most recent text.

"Ugh, it says she finally figured out how she wants to use her right to do whatever she wants with me... I thought she'd forgotten..."

Back when Shiren fought Kiyomizu, she'd promised her the right to do whatever she wanted to him to shut her up.

"What on Earth...? Why now...?"

"Your service is appreciated, Ryouta..."

"Well, the stuff with Kiyomizu will work out somehow, probably... She's super strong, and she can be mature when she wants to be. You know, I'm more worried about my sister, who's an *actual* adult... I haven't seen her at all lately..."

He hadn't seen her even once. Come to think of it, the last time he *had* seen her was when she'd snuck into his apartment and gotten shocked. She'd seemed so *her*, he'd assumed she'd show up again in no time.

"I think it's unlikely," said Ryouta, "but you don't think she actually died somewhere out there, do you...? She's come close so many times, I don't know what she could have possibly gotten herself into."

"I'm sure she's all right, but...have you tried contacting her?"

"Yeah, but she hasn't responded to my messages."

His inbox was still filled with Kiyomizu's name.

"She's probably fine... And I *have* worried about her a million times in the past, and even when it seems like there's no way she could recover, she's survived every time..."

Thinking about it wasn't going to help, so he decided to give the topic a rest for the moment.

"Well, I suppose there are a few exceptions, but things are essentially the same as before," Sasara said, turning to look ahead.

For whatever reason, Ouka and Alfoncina had started singing an *enka* duet.

(Ouka) Oh, the snow in Yamagata ♪
(Alfoncina) Is colder than it's ever been ♪
(Ouka) I wish you would've said no ♪
(Alfoncina) Because now you've given me hope ♪
(Ouka) Once the cherries start blooming ♪
(Alfoncina) Maybe my ice will start to melt ♪
(Both) Oh, this is Higashine love ♪

"They're actually pretty good at *enka*...," said Ryouta.

"I have a feeling it won't be long before everything is back the way it was."

"I guess so... Or maybe we're just stuck, unable to move forward..."

"Perhaps that's not a bad thing. My job is to keep the peace in the Empire, after all. It's important that some things stay the same."

"You know, that's nice to hear, Sasara."

Ryouta himself had stood up to Sairi in order to keep the things around him from changing.

"I only said what I was thinking. To be honest, I wish for things to be even more peaceful, for us to have the freedom to go back and forth across the border as we please. What we have right now is not peace—it is simply a state of no conflict. I will continue to wield my blade and fight for that purpose, even in the face of a powerful enemy like Sairi. I take pride in this resolve."

"Wow..."

Ryouta was at a loss for words—he was genuinely touched. Sasara had spoken without hesitation, even after the horrible injuries she'd sustained in her fight with Sairi.

"You're really something, Sasara."

"What does that mean? I-if you're trying to butter me up, you won't get anything out of me..."

In the face of his earnest praise, Sasara flushed and seemed to lose her cool.

"No, I mean it. You're incredible. You really do have an eye on the future."

"I have to go to Japan, too, you know, so I do not want the border to remain closed forever."

She rummaged around for something in her bag.

"There are plenty of establishments I have my eye on. I'll only have enough free time to visit two during this trip."

"Hmm…? What do you mean by 'establishments'…?"

"Ah, here it is." Sasara pulled out a book.

Top 50 Best Ramen Spots in Oshiro

"That's what you're after?!"

"Didn't you know? There is a district called Nagase in the north of Oshiro, and it is considered one of the hottest ramen battlegrounds in Japan. There are lines at every restaurant in the area, and the most well-known have even opened branches in Tokyo."

"I'm aware, as a former resident of Oshiro, but I've never been out there."

"You're missing out on seventy percent of life."

"So ramen is seventy percent of life to you?"

"I will not be able to visit Nagase this time around, but I believe I can make it to both Oojirou and Kegon. I wish I could go to Fujimoto-ke, too, but I believe there will be a line, so it'd be a bit tight time-wise, don't you think?"

"Please don't ask me—I have no idea."

"Oojirou's specialty is their chicken *char siu*. The soup uses a soy-sauce base and is stuffed with little chicken *char siu* and scallions—an odd sight, indeed. Unlike normal pork *char siu*, chicken *char siu* tastes sweeter the longer you chew on it. By contrast, Kegon is known for stuffing their bowls with a large volume of thinly sliced onion and for adding cheese, of course. Fujimoto-ke is yet another of those house-style places, but I hear the spinach is quite unique—"

It sounded like Sasara's idea of "peace" was eating ramen.

"Ramen aside, I agree completely that peace is important. I want a world where everyone has a smile on their face." Ryouta gripped the scabbard at his belt. "You can't carry your sword with you now because you're injured, right? So no matter what happens, I'll fight in your place."

"Ha. You may not be able to fight, but at least you can talk."

It sounded as though she was poking fun at him, but her expression was bright.

"I'll work hard to fight both as Ouka's minion *and* as a part of her guard," Ryouta replied enthusiastically.

No matter what happened in the future, he would always be Ouka's minion.

"Ah yes. Organizationally speaking..." Sasara's expression suddenly clouded over. "By the way, a thought just occurred to me..."

"What is it?"

"This is...a bit awkward to ask, but..."

Sasara's face went red, and she squirmed. She kept glancing at Ryouta, looking away, then glancing back again over and over as though she couldn't make up her mind.

"Seriously, what is it...?" asked Ryouta.

"Have you...um...*deepened* your relationship with Lady Ouka...?"

Ryouta immediately went bright red. "Don't ask me things like that! And Ouka's just over there..."

"But y-you love each other, no? Then...that would be the natural conclusion... I doubt you would ever forget the day you decided to c-cross the line together..."

"Sasara, come here."

This wasn't something he could say out loud. He had to whisper it to her.

"O-okay...?" Sasara, face still flushed, leaned over to Ryouta.

"Listen. We've done, uh...nothing. We haven't even kissed."

"What...? You've been living together for quite some time now, haven't you?"

"Hey, could you talk a little quieter...? You're right, though... We *have* been living together for a while. Like, two or three days I could understand, but..."

"I—I do not understand... It sounds like there is a problem..."

Now Sasara was faltering for a whole new reason.

"You think so, too, right…? But things just never go in that direction, or she's just never in the mood…"

Pain suddenly shot through Ryouta's cheeks. Sasara had pinched him. Hard.

"Um, Sasara? That hurts…"

That put an end to their whispered conversation, and they pulled apart.

"I grew irritated listening to you. My apologies."

"If you're sorry, could you please stop pinching me…?"

"You are so unreliable, I am starting to question my own decisions! You need to give everyone a reason to give up; otherwise, *you* will be the one crying over the ensuing bloodbath!"

"Wh-what are you talking about…?"

"To put it simply, your decisions never bring peace—they are unreliable and risky! Always!" Finally, Sasara dropped her hand and stopped pinching him. "You will die if you do not hurry up and settle down."

"Whoa… That's kind of extreme… But I guess I get what you mean…"

Ryouta had been gravely injured in almost every encounter thus far. It happened so often that he couldn't even be bothered to keep count anymore.

"You had best take care not to get injured again today."

"What? We're going for dinner. Why would I get injured? Nothing's going to happen."

There wasn't going to be any mortal combat at a dinner party. At least, that's what Ryouta thought.

"I hope so." Sasara looked down at Ryouta's sword and knit her brows. "But remember, there are times when one must draw one's blade in order to preserve peace."

Their bus arrived at the specified hotel without incident.

The meeting would be taking place in the restaurant on the top floor, and hotel employees, dressed in suits, escorted them to the elevator.

There were not very many visitors from the old Empire attending the dinner, and all of them managed to fit in one elevator. Only a few of their accompanying guards had to go up separately.

A view of the surrounding area was visible through a glass window in the elevator. They could see the city of Oshiro below and the mountains separating it from the old Empire.

"I guess this is it," Ryouta murmured as he took in the sight.

I hope Shiren's doing okay.

The mountains weren't even that tall, the forests not even that deep, yet it felt as though they lived in completely different worlds.

Please be okay, Shiren.

But if she wasn't—

—he didn't have an answer for that yet.

The high-speed elevator reached the top floor in no time at all.

"I have been awaiting your arrival."

As they stepped out of the elevator, a girl greeted them, speaking gently and politely. For a moment, Ryouta thought this was a member of the Holy Sacred Blood Empire sent to receive them. But as he realized who it was, he began to doubt his eyes.

It was Shiren, wearing an elegant dress.

It wasn't gaudy or covered with glittering gemstones, but it made her look like a refined noblewoman. The ornament in her hair made her seem even more grown-up.

If someone told him this wasn't Shiren after all, he'd probably believe them. The impression she was giving off was completely different than when she'd lived in the old Empire.

"Thank you so much for taking the time to visit today. I am Shiren the First, ruler of the Holy Sacred Blood Empire." Shiren bowed gracefully.

"You look like an emperor."

Just as those words left Ryouta's mouth, he realized how weird a thing it was to say.

"Oh, right. That's because you *are* an emperor."

This wasn't the girl he used to share a roof with.

What was I worried about? She's doing fine. Better than fine.

But...

...soon, however, another thought came to Ryouta's mind.

She looks kind of lonely, though...

Ouka's

Heroine Danger Rating!

Shiren   Danger: ★★★★★
I want to get rid of her as quickly as possible, whatever it takes.

Sasara   Danger: ★★★★☆
She's actually a big risk, so I want to get rid of her as quickly as possible, too.

Kimura   Danger: ★★★☆☆
I think she should be fine, but there is a risk of her rebounding with little warning.

Tamaki   Danger: ☆☆☆☆☆
I figure some invisible force will keep her in check. I'll just ignore her.

EPISODE 4
LET'S ALL GO HOME TO THE EMPIRE!

The entire party was brought to their table and took their seats.

Those from the old Empire sat by the window, and those from the Holy Sacred Blood Empire sat opposite them.

Ouka sat in the middle, with Alfoncina to her right and Ryouta to her left. Kokoko sat to the right of Alfoncina, and Sasara sat to the left of Ryouta. Due to space limitations, Tamaki was seated at a separate table some distance away.

On the opposite side, Emperor Shiren sat in the middle, with Archbishop Sairi and a male executive from the organization to her right and left. A few in attendance were wearing clothes that looked a lot like Kiyomizu's, so some of them were likely from the order of the Virginal Father.

"To my right is Archbishop New Progenitor Alfoncina, and to my left is Bishop Kyousuke Tamura."

"This is Alfoncina the Thirteenth on my right, and my minion, Ryouta Sarano, on my left."

Both sides began to courteously introduce their attendees.

Sairi, or New Progenitor Alfoncina, wore a mostly white dress like her daughter. Since she was the archbishop, Ryouta had thought she might wear something weird like a modified priestess outfit, but that turned out not to be the case. Apparently, that attire was an old Empire original.

She hardly seemed like Shiren's mother—she looked young and not at all like a powerful swordsman.

Objectively, this looked like nothing more than a social gathering, but Ryouta was still on edge.

Why are Shiren and Ouka so formal with each other...? It's making me really uncomfortable...

Neither of them seemed to be playing around—they were both acting like rulers. The mood was making it impossible to relax.

"The purpose of this meeting is to forge a friendly relationship with our neighboring nation, the old Empire." Shiren began her opening statements as representative of the new Empire. "Everyone, I would like for you to think about the syllables that make up the word *tomato. To. Ma. To.* Whether you recite them forward or backward, they still sound like *tomato.* Life is very much the same. You may think it has come to an end, when in fact you have come across a new beginning. At the same time, a beginning signals the end of something else. What I mean to say is that, um… Uh, tomatoes are… Tomatoes are great."

Her attempt to say something clever ended in failure.

Looks aside, it seems like she's still the same Shiren…

"All right, everyone. I propose a toast to the prosperity of tomatoes!"

"Shouldn't you toast to the prosperity of your country instead?!" Ryouta couldn't help but interject. Regardless, the toast went on as normal.

"Our first dish is soup. It will be a soup with shark fin and bird's nest—"

He had expected nothing less of a meal held between the leaders of two countries. They were apparently getting some seriously high-class soup.

"—with tomato."

"Could you not put tomatoes in with such fancy ingredients?!"

"Watch your table manners, Ryouta," Ouka warned him politely.

It seemed like interjections were not going to be tolerated here.

"S-sorry… Damn, things are so different from usual, it's wearing on me…" Ryouta had begun to stand out in a bad way.

"Both of our respective nations have quite a lot of problems, don't they? Your Holy Majesty, is there any policy you believe needs to be implemented right away?"

"Yes. Within the next six months, I plan on having the number of tomatoes used in chain burger joints doubled. Ultimately, I would like to increase the amount fivefold in five years' time."

"Wow, what a *pointless* policy! And don't you think increasing the amount of tomato by five times would ruin the burger's balance?!"

©Hiroki Ozaki

"Ryouta, please do not say things that would embarrass our country," Ouka warned him politely again.

"In that case, please stop saying things that are practically *begging* for my commentary…"

The conversation certainly sounded formal, but the subjects being discussed were so absurd that it was stressing Ryouta out.

"Ah, yes. Would Your Majesty like to hear the national anthem of our new nation?"

"I would be delighted."

"Would the staff please play the song?"

Holy Sacred Blood Empire National Anthem

Tomatomatomatomato Tomatomatomatomato
Red like the sun   Red like a mailbox
Red like our blood   Red like the sun
(Spoken) But my face turns even redder when I'm with you
Tomatomatomatomato Tomatomatomatomato
Tomatomatomatomato Tomatomatomatomato

"Why is there a spoken part?! It sounds so dumb! And you have *red like the sun* twice! Couldn't you think of any more similes?! At least sing a little more about the country itself!"

"Ryouta, do not nitpick other countries' anthems."

"Minion, I would advise against irritating Her Majesty any further than you already have."

"Ouka, Shiren, can we stop with this joke now…? I'm suffocating…"

Ryouta was truly alone with no one to help him.

"Ah, yes. I have heard that Your Holy Majesty has been hard at work studying."

"I have. I often procrastinated in the past, but I have decided to put in a bit more effort. At present, I am studying Italian history."

"Italian history! Home of the Roman Empire—as a ruler, I believe that's perfect. You will have a lot to learn from them. May I ask what sorts of things you've learned?"

Ryouta was curious, too.

Is she actually studying? If she is, that's some amazing progress. Maybe she developed some self-awareness when she became emperor.

"Long ago, there was the Roman Empire. Then there was the Renaissance. Now we have Italy. The end."

"That's way too abbreviated!" Unsurprisingly, she hadn't improved at all. "There has to be something between the Roman Empire and the Renaissance!"

"Tomatoes, meat, onions, salami…"

"That's what you put between buns in a burger!"

"I never thought I would hear the word *Renaissance* come out of my Shiren's mouth… She has truly grown!" Sairi sounded almost moved.

"Even elementary school kids know what the Renaissance is! Your standards are way too low!"

"I was able to learn the word after writing it a hundred times in my notebook, Mom."

"It's not something you need to work *that* hard to remember!"

"I even know the difference between the Renaissance and a balsamic vinaigrette."

"How do you mix those two up?!"

"My, I've developed quite the craving for pizza after all this talk about Italy. Excuse me, could I add on an order of pizza to our dinner? Large, please."

"Are you allowed to order a pizza during a full-course meal?!"

Even Sairi was making sensational statements now.

"If you can't make it, then you may order one in. Oh, I'll have a side of fried chicken, too."

"I'm begging you, please do not order a pizza delivery during a full-course meal! This is a diplomatic meeting between two nations!"

"I'll have the rest of the dishes in the meal, too, of course. As they say, there is always extra room for dessert."

"You didn't order dessert! Pizza isn't dessert!"

Both mother and daughter were a little off their rocker, and Ryouta couldn't help calling them out. As a result, he was the only one falling behind on his meal.

"Oh, are you not hungry, minion? In that case, I will have what you do not eat."

"Shiren, you might be trying to sound polite, but you're still trying to steal my food…"

At last, Ryouta resumed eating, which gave him a chance to steal a look at Shiren.

She's been sounding different, but I think she's still having fun…

The emperor persona she'd been trying to force didn't really suit her, but she didn't seem too lonely or upset.

In fact, after all the anxiety he'd suffered on the way here, Ryouta felt a little bit let down.

Ouka also seemed keen on playing the part of emperor and had no intentions of treating Shiren as a younger sister. She didn't have anything negative to say about the new Empire at all.

The gathering was shaping up to be no more than what it was on the surface—a meal held between two nations.

Is that it, then?

If Shiren had accepted her new position, then that was a good thing.

If he went up to someone he thought was happy and told them they were actually miserable, it would just make him a meddling busybody.

I just wish we could've interacted like we used to.

Why was she calling him "minion" anyway? She could just call him "Ryouta" like normal, couldn't she? Shiren wasn't letting any of their past relationship come to the surface at all.

She wasn't even calling Ouka "Big Sis." But then Ouka wasn't treating her like a sister, either.

This might be a diplomatic function, but there's no need for them to act like they're not even related.

Even Ryouta knew that was selfish of him, though. Happiness wasn't a zero-sum game, where one person's happiness came at the cost of someone else's. Sometimes, you had to accept compromise and find contentment somewhere else.

Please find your happiness, Shiren. And I'll try my best as Ouka's minion.

Besides, there was nothing grim about the mood at the table. Even the executives from the order of the Virginal Father had started drinking and were growing tipsy.

Time flew by, and soon, it was time for dessert—sweet tomato sorbet. It sounded like a weird dish, but it turned out to be a pretty standard dessert.

I guess it'll be over soon. Well, I guess if things are going this amicably between them, we'll probably see each other again sometime...

Ryouta decided to savor every bite as slowly as possible. He wanted to stay here as long as he could.

He stole a glance at Shiren. At the same time, Shiren just happened to look at Ryouta.

Oh—

For the first time in a long while, she was meeting his eyes.

But tragically, Ryouta had *no idea* what was going on in Shiren's head.

I've read manga where two people look at each other and know exactly how the other feels, but I guess it isn't like that in reality...

He wouldn't know unless she told him.

For the briefest moment, she smiled at him, but it was an emperor's smile.

There's no way I could be of any help to a foreign nation's ruler. Even if she asked, there's nothing I can do...

Ryouta, feeling unnecessary, slowly finished his sorbet.

I guess we'll be going home soon.

The meeting had ended much too quickly.

Why couldn't he be satisfied that it'd gone smoothly? He didn't have the words to explain how he felt.

But then the chocolate cake arrived.

"Right, there are two desserts. I guess that happens sometimes."

He decided to enjoy it, since it meant his time with Shiren had been extended.

Five minutes later, plates of *kuzumochi* were brought out.

Then came sesame *dango*.

Then there was a serving of cheesecake.

Then a massive chocolate parfait.

"How many desserts are there?!"

This was no longer the time to be lamenting their impending separation.

"I coordinated the dessert menu." Sairi raised her hand. "See, I was being considerate. I wanted to delay your good-byes for as long as possible. And they say there's always more room for dessert."

"You came up with that excuse just now, didn't you?! Besides, with this much dessert, I think we've more than filled that 'extra room'!"

A powerful negative aura washed over them from the next table over.

"E-e-excuse me... I ate too much, and now I feel sick... Where might I find the washroom...? Bleh..."

Tamaki was about to throw up again.

"You look awful, Shijou!"

"I figured I have no right to leave any leftovers, so I did what I could to eat everything, but I seem to be at my limit... I'm not often allowed to eat this much food..."

"Wow, your homelife sounds depressing."

"I have a small stomach...and a small spirit... Hee-hee..."

"Try to stay positive, okay?!"

"Oh, but there's still mango pudding and coconut milk to eat," Sairi piped up.

"She's already full!" Ryouta yelled back.

In the end, there were another five dishes before dessert was over.

"*Phew...* I think we're finally done..."

All Ryouta had done was eat, but he still felt exhausted.

"We will be returning to the Sacred Blood Empire, then. Your Holy Majesty, thank you for inviting us here today." Ouka courteously gave her thanks to Shiren.

"Ah, there's one last thing I would like to address," Shiren replied.

She was both kind and dignified, befitting her position as emperor. The childish Shiren Ryouta used to know was nowhere to be seen.

"Oh? What is it?"

"Mom." This time, Shiren turned to Sairi. "It was with your help that I became emperor and received the opportunity to act as the leader of many Sacred Blooded. I believe now we can work together amicably with the Sacred Blood Empire to protect our people. No words are enough to thank you."

"Oh my. You sound like a different person, Shiren."

If even Sairi felt the need to point that out, then what Shiren was saying must really be unnatural.

"I'm certain that had I remained in the old Empire in Akinomiya, I would have stayed complacent and never learned anything. I am truly, truly thankful."

Sairi brought a hand to her mouth, moved by Shiren's impeccable words of gratitude.

"Which is why I think the Holy Sacred Blood Empire will be just fine in your hands."

"What?"

A shocking revelation had been mixed in with Shiren's words.

She slowly bowed her head.

"I will be defecting to the old Empire."

Sairi's expression froze. There was still a smile on her face, but even Ryouta could see she had been blindsided.

"What a strange thing to say, Shiren…"

"It's not strange. I am the emperor. I am the most powerful and most important person in this country. I should be allowed to leave."

Her tone of voice had shifted back to how Ryouta remembered it from before.

A stir moved through the new Empire's executives.

"Shiren, if your work as emperor is too overwhelming, you can always take a break. Feel free to take it easy."

"I'm not taking a break. I'm going home." Shiren turned to look at Ouka again. Her mouth was drawn in a tight, thin line.

"If there's something you want to say, then say it," said Ouka.

"Big Sis! I want to go back to the Empire! I was bored here after three days! I would have been fine just seeing my mom every once in a while!"

At last, Shiren had admitted how she truly felt.

"What on Earth are you saying? You said yourself you didn't care if you never came back." Ouka awkwardly looked away. "Ryouta's my minion now... You can't rewind time."

"I know. I'm not trying to. Ryouta's your minion; he belongs to the ruler of the Sacred Blood Empire."

Relief washed over Ouka's face.

"But Ryouta was my minion once. You can't change that, either. That's all I need."

Shiren gave Ouka a genuine smile. There was a majesty about her that Ryouta had never seen before.

"You can't just keep going back and trying again, Shiren. Did you think the decision you made a month ago was just for fun?"

When Shiren left the Sacred Blood Empire, Ouka had told her to steel her resolve. Everyone believed she had done just that.

"I know."

"You don't. It's well within my right to reject the return of a former citizen, you know? All you did was announce your own defection. I never agreed to take you back."

"Sure. If I didn't have any power, that's probably how it would have turned out." Shiren remained calm, despite the absurdity of her statement. "But I am asking you a favor, as emperor of the Holy Sacred Blood Empire."

Ouka, on the other hand, looked exasperated.

Shiren wasn't just rushing ahead like she'd always done before. She had readied her most powerful card to challenge Ouka.

This was negotiation. This was diplomacy.

"Big Sis, you said I didn't have any do-overs, right? I'm not planning on doing anything over. I've learned so much here in the new Empire. I even learned that I can't stay here forever. And that is why I'm making the choice to leave."

The Shiren in front of her now was most certainly different than the one Ouka had known before. She might as well have been someone else entirely. The old Shiren would have never said anything like this.

Perhaps, in a way, she *had* grown. Maybe.

"I was hoping to establish diplomatic relations with you, if possible. I want the rules for entering the Empire from the Holy Sacred Blood Empire—Japan, essentially—to be loosened in steps. Then I can see my mom. The Sacred Blooded seem to be reconciling. You can't remain closed off forever, you know."

"You know you don't have any real power, right...?"

"Maybe not. But I *am* emperor. No one else in the Holy Sacred Blood Empire has Imperial blood like me. If I go over to your side, I should be worth using."

Ouka clicked her tongue. At some point, they'd found themselves sitting at the negotiation table.

She'd never had any intention of allowing Shiren to come home. And yet Shiren was now staring back at her boldly. Not only that, but she'd also acknowledged that Ryouta was Ouka's minion.

After that, Ouka couldn't turn around and say she didn't want Shiren to come back. That would be admitting she was still terrified Shiren might take Ryouta away from her. And her pride would never allow her to say that out loud.

"Very well. I'll allow you to return. But..."

The match was essentially set at that point. Ouka was much too kind to wield her power irrationally. She couldn't keep abandoning her little sister like that.

"What about you, Ryouta? Are you okay with this?" Shiren asked.

"I'm just Ouka's minion, so I'll do what she says... You'd beat me up if I really said that, wouldn't you?"

For the first time, unease crossed Shiren's face. Her expression was fragile, like she had given up on everything.

When facing Ouka, she had used logic, pushing aside her feelings as she moved the conversation along. But she couldn't do that with Ryouta.

Even though she knew her own emotions, there was no way to tell what others felt. She didn't know what Ryouta was thinking or feeling.

"Shiren, I'm not your minion anymore. You're not my master. I'm not wearing your collar."

He was only stating the obvious. So why did it hurt her heart so much to hear it?

"If I had to, I'd say we're…" Ryouta looked into Shiren's frightened eyes. "…friends."

There was nothing about the word that warranted embarrassment. It was the perfect word to describe their relationship.

"F-friends…" Shiren's face flushed redder and redder in bashfulness.

"Come on, then. I'm not serving you anymore, but I'll help you as a friend." Ryouta extended a hand.

"It's good to be home, Ryouta." Shiren reached out to take it.

Things weren't going back to the way they were, but this wasn't half-bad, either.

But…

"I won't let that happen."

…Sairi's stern voice stopped Shiren in her tracks.

"The adult world runs on set schedules. I'm sorry, but I can't allow this."

"Mom, I'll be back. I'm just changing where I live."

"I don't believe you! I can't stand the thought of being apart from you again, Shiren!" Sairi yelled like a child. "I don't know what will happen to you if we end up separated again… I left you behind, and then I didn't see you for years… I don't want to let you go ever again!"

Sairi, too, was painfully acquainted with the agony of being apart from someone she loved. Of course she would be afraid of going through that again.

And Shiren didn't have the courage to ignore her. Because she understood.

Her hand reaching out toward Ryouta's came to a halt.

Slowly, she turned to look at Sairi. There was a vague smile on her face.

"I wasn't sure how things were going to turn out, but I thought this might happen. I could…never leave you behind, Mom."

This is my limit, Shiren thought.

If there was only one Shiren, she had to stay by her mother.

"Thank you, Shiren…" Sairi slowly reached out toward her daughter.

"I'm sorry, everyone," Shiren spoke, her back to the old Empire side. "I'm not going with you. I can't stay a child forever. I have to grow up. But I've told you how I felt. Please know that those feelings are genuine."

Her hand entwined with another.

Ryouta's.

"What?"

Her head whirled around. And there he was—her old minion.

It was so sudden, no one understood what happened. Shiren looked to Ryouta with disbelief written all over her face. Earnest eyes stared straight back at her.

"H-how rude of you, Ryouta… Wh-why are you being so self—?"

"I can't help it. You said you told us how you felt, right?"

"Yeah, what about it…?"

"You told us you wanted to come home with us. And so I acted."

"But I *just said* I can't go back! You don't understand *anything*!"

Shiren was genuinely furious. She had been through so much pain because she couldn't act on her feelings—did Ryouta not understand that?

"I didn't just hear the words you said with your mouth. I heard the words from your heart, too."

"What?"

Ryouta gave a firm nod. "Your desperate desire to go home reached me. That's my power as your minion—to feel my master's feelings."

"Y-you don't mean—" Shiren didn't believe it at first.

She didn't think she'd ever managed to make Ryouta her minion, not fully.

"So my legs moved on their own, and I grabbed your hand. That's why I said I couldn't help it. You called for me."

Ryouta gave her a brilliant smile.

Shiren wished she could look away, but she couldn't.

"You said you've grown up, right, Shiren?"

"Y-yes…"

"But making a decision because someone told you what to do doesn't sound very grown-up."

"…"

"An adult would choose for herself how she wants to live. What do *you* want to do?"

Shiren's eyes widened. If she didn't give the correct answer right now, history would only repeat itself.

©Hiroki Ozaki

Silence settled over the room.

Everyone probably had things they wanted to say, but no one had time to butt in before Shiren answered.

"I want to go back." Shiren formed each word carefully as she spoke. There was strength in her eyes, as though she was ready for the fight ahead.

"All right. And because I'm your minion, I'll make that happen," Ryouta replied with a smile.

Sairi looked like she'd just been robbed.

Ouka's expression remained unchanged. She was merely observing the scene as it unfolded.

Shiren slowly turned to look at Sairi, letting go of Ryouta's hand.

"I'm leaving, Mom."

"You are not."

"Try and stop me."

Shiren had known this would come down to a test of strength. If she was truly powerless, she would never have the chance to obtain her own happiness.

And that was why she intended to fight back with everything she had.

"Very well, new order of the Virginal Father, stop Shiren! Show her what the executive class can do!" Sairi roared out her orders.

"Ma'am, I'm sorry…but…"

"Bishop Tamura? What is it?"

"We ate so much, we can barely move…"

Apparently, they had gorged themselves on the food, and none of them were prepared for this.

"I could barely fit the dessert myself…"

"Sheesh! You should be able to handle that much easily! And we were planning on ramen for the after-party!"

It sounded like Sairi's stomach was a bottomless pit.

"I wish we could have gone to the after-party… We rarely ever come to Japan… If only I had an hour of free time…"

"Sasara! The ramen isn't the important part here!"

The order of the Virginal Father was now severely limited in what it could do.

"But team Akinomiya didn't bring much in the way of security, did they? I doubt your guards are fully healed from our last fight."

Sairi was still confident in her power. This was her home turf. She wasn't going to lose.

Even though the executives of the order seemed dazed from overeating, they still took up their fighting positions.

"And what, exactly, were you planning on doing without any input from your emperor, Ryouta?" Ouka stared at him coolly.

"Oh, Ouka—"

"I said I would take in the defector, but I don't recall ever saying I would fight for her."

A shadow fell over Shiren's face. Ouka hadn't promised to help them, but she and Ryouta could not win alone.

"However, I will act upon a request made by another national leader. I am willing to deploy my soldiers in order to suppress a revolt." Ouka sounded genuinely annoyed.

"Thanks, Big Sis!" Shiren shouted, her eyes sparkling.

"Don't get the wrong idea. This is all for my country's profit. And my grandstanding minion will not be receiving pay for a while." Ouka glared at Ryouta.

"Lady Ouka, I'm sorry, but…I don't think I'll be able to fight due to my injuries…" Sasara came to Ouka's side and apologized.

"Don't worry; you may rest, Sasara. You didn't even bring your weapon today."

"But we don't have enough people."

"Yes, we do. Look at them. This will be an easy fight."

A lone swordsman came to stand before the order of the Virginal Father.

"It will be so. I, Masatsuna Toraha, shall emerge victorious."

Masatsuna Toraha was said to be the most powerful swordsman in the Empire. He was also Sasara's cousin, and he had once faced Ryouta in a serious battle.

"I should hope so. And when you do, I'll give you the right to marry whoever you like as your prize."

"Your Majesty… A-are you sure…?" Toraha flushed.

"Wait! That cannot be his prize! Pick something a little more uninspiring, please!"

"I suppose you're right. Maybe I should narrow his choices to only someone he's related to."

"That's even worse!" Sasara was on the verge of tears.

"I can handle this. I—I can take these guys i-in an instant if I just stay c-calm."

"You're not calm at all. Are you okay? Though I guess you're powerful enough you don't need to stay calm."

Toraha held his wooden training sword at the ready. "A real blade would be wasted on an enemy such as this... Yah!"

He closed the distance between them in an instant and jabbed all the men from the order in the stomach.

"Bluh—" "I'm gonna—" "Where's the bathroom?!"

The bloated executives quickly left the scene.

"No one could fight in such a condition. Fools."

He was right; no one should be fighting on a full stomach.

"But you got through dessert," Ryouta said. "Guess you're secretly a big eater."

Even Ryouta was finally feeling the effects of all that dessert.

"Well, I had everything I couldn't eat wrapped up so I could take it home," replied Toraha. "Despite our history, my family is poor. We cannot afford to waste food..."

"A victory for the thrifty, I suppose..."

With that, all the enemies aside from Sairi were out of the picture. But this was Sairi's stronghold.

"I'm impressed. But you can only fell so many enemies with your sword alone."

Members of the order of the Virginal Father soon flooded the room—there must have been a hundred of them.

"Where were all these people hiding? This makes no sense." Ouka was amazed by their sheer number.

"But this is how many I needed."

"Um... I'll do my best to keep fighting, but...I don't think the circumstances are in my favor with this many of them..." Toraha was already giving up.

"I suppose so. Then I will simply have to call in reinforcements," said Ouka, calm as ever. She'd seemed much more troubled earlier, when talking to Shiren. "We'll fight fire with fire. All right, you can come out now."

Shwump.

Several people dressed in all black descended on the members of the order. By the time they looked up, it was already too late.

At some point, an entire group of people dressed in black had affixed themselves to the ceiling.

As soon as they dropped down, the fight began.

"Well, things have certainly escalated... Is this my fault...?" Shiren recoiled slightly. She hadn't anticipated a fight involving this many people.

"Goodness. All this chaos because one girl wanted to be selfish."

One of those dressed in black peeled off her mask.

Kiyomizu Jouryuuji stood before Shiren with annoyance on her face.

"Sorry...," replied Shiren. "I didn't think about what effect it would have..."

"What are you apologizing for? You wouldn't have made this decision if you were worried about causing trouble. You did what you thought was right, so own it."

"I owe you so much."

"If I wasn't getting anything out of this, I wouldn't be doing it! Either way, we need to beat this new order of the Virginal Father into submission!"

Voices yelling "Don't underestimate the Jouryuuji family!" could be heard from the direction of the brawl. It seemed a number of people from the exiled Jouryuuji clan were partaking in the fight.

"This will take a little time. I'll leave the rest to you all."

And with that, Kiyomizu moved to dive back into the fight.

But just before she did, she turned around one last time.

"Ryouta dearest, I'm going to use my right to have you do whatever I wish right now!"

"Wait, now...?"

"Yes. There was never a rule that I couldn't use it in a fight." She looked at Ryouta smugly. "Let me tell you before I go back in."

"Uh, okay… Go ahead…"

"Make Shiren happy! And if you don't, I'll sue you for breach of contract!"

Ryouta couldn't believe his ears. Kiyomizu had used her one free pass on him not for herself, but for Shiren.

"Hey, has someone brainwashed you or something? Are you actually Kiyomizu's twin?"

"How rude! I would punch you if you weren't my Ryouta dearest." She huffed, pouting. "I was never going to use my pass to keep you for myself. What's the point if I don't seduce you with my own charm?!"

"Y-you…really are nice to your friends…"

Ryouta was seriously impressed.

"She and I aren't friends! We're rivals!"

And with that, Kiyomizu leaped back into the fight with the new order of the Virginal Father.

"Well. It seems they'll be settling that matter among themselves." Ouka took a step forward—toward Sairi's side.

"Your Imperial Majesty of the old Empire, I think it's time you return to Akinomiya," said Sairi. One of her underlings brought her a sword. She grasped it silently. "At the end of the day, the strongest member of this organization is me. Though I *do* wish the others would try a little harder sometimes…"

"If you're getting serious, then I suppose I must do the same." Ouka turned to Ryouta. "Come here, Ryouta. You have a more important role than wielding a sword."

"What?"

He approached, and Ouka ripped into his arm with her teeth.

"Ow—!"

Blood oozed from the wound.

"Better than a fight to the death, no? Deal with it. You are my minion."

Ouka quietly lapped up the blood.

Pure-white wings of light unfurled from her back. Judging by the color alone, they looked like angel wings, but a terrifying aura emanated from them, like that of a devil risen from the earth.

"You're like the Goddess of Blood," Sairi said flatly.

"Your ancestors, too, worshipped this form. I never thought I'd be fighting a descendant of the first archbishop, but I suppose this is destiny."

Rights to the Imperial throne were not maintained by tradition, but by pure power. The Imperial family was not merely of noble birth, and their station was not symbolic.

"I will show you what it means to make an enemy of the Sarano family."

"You know, I've always wanted to face you in battle." Sairi drew her sword.

The first one to attack was Ouka. She closed the distance between them in a blink of an eye. Her nails had transformed into the sharp claws of a beast. These were not just for ripping flesh—they could also tear a person in half.

Sairi faced those claws with tranquility, sword in hand. She wouldn't strike yet. It was much too dangerous to engage before knowing how the enemy would attack.

Sairi had made it through life essentially undefeated, but that was because her fighting style emphasized defense. She did not expose herself to risk. She only attacked when she was safe.

It was almost impossible to break down the defenses of a human on her level. All she had to do was wait thirty minutes, or an hour at most, until her opponent started showing signs of weakness.

If it looked like she was one-sidedly attacking, that was only proof of how much less skilled her opponent was.

This time, too, her defensive tactics were successful.

Mouths appeared in Ouka's wings and bared fangs. Her claws were just the opening act. *This* was the real deal.

The mouths aimed for Sairi's shoulder. She could have blocked them with her sword, but—

This is bad!

—Sairi decided to leap backward.

The darkened mouths stretched forward, as though they had a will of their own, chasing Sairi. They scraped against her shoulder, and it didn't feel like a bite. Instead, it was like she'd been touched by dry ice. Blood streamed from the wound, but it wasn't that deep.

"I was right to pull back," said Sairi. "You would have ripped my head clean off if I hadn't."

"It seems seventy percent of your skill is animal instinct."

At a distance of thirty meters, they laughed at each other.

"I figured if I blocked with my sword, they'd simply eat it."

"A good assumption. It's practically impossible to physically block these wings."

There was majestic dignity to Ouka's countenance.

"According to my own rules, I only use my power when I need to. Most things can be solved with this level of force, but doing that would make me a complete dictator, wouldn't it?"

"I'd expect no less from the Goddess of Blood's power."

"No one would pray to her if she wasn't powerful. Unless the one in authority is insurmountably strong, people only grow jealous and resentful."

"Indeed. But thanks to you showing your hand so quickly, I can tell that your absolute power isn't so absolute." Sairi's expression grew confident.

Ouka frowned and clicked her tongue. "What level are you operating on...?"

Shiren stood still, watching the fight, but not because she was frozen with fear. This battle would determine her destiny, and she couldn't afford to run or look away. Even if she managed to escape, it wouldn't make a difference if they couldn't stop Sairi.

Since she wasn't running, her friend Ryouta stayed by her side. She was no longer his master, but he still had to do what he could to keep his friend safe.

I'm not sure if I can actually protect her, though...

As much as he hated to admit it, there was no space in the battle unfolding before him for superficial power. If he thoughtlessly stepped in, he would immediately die. He wanted to help, but there was nothing he could do.

"It's time to finish this."

Sairi pulled back her sword, then thrust it toward Ouka like a spear. She closed in on Ouka like it was nothing, like she herself was a bullet fired from a gun. The expression on Ouka's face said she knew she was in trouble.

Though she was borrowing her ancestors' powers, there was only so much Ouka could do in the face of changing momentum. She was helpless before such a rapid approach.

Big Sis!

Shiren was about to shout, but before she could, Ouka was sent flying.

All the leftover plates on the table clattered to the floor.

"Ouka!"

Once his head caught up with the awful sight, Ryouta finally found his voice to call out.

There was no way Ouka would walk away from that thrust unharmed. In fact, it was hard to believe she'd even survive.

That was why, when he saw Ouka sit up, he felt relief wash over him.

"That's…only a replica of your regular sword…"

"Yes. This *was* just a friendly get-together, after all."

A replica wouldn't even be able to pierce her skin.

"You're taking me for a fool…"

"You would have died if this had been my real sword, you know."

Ouka had nothing to say in response. She was alive because Sairi had spared her.

"You are the emperor, and we need you as part of our plan for the new Empire. I cannot afford to kill you. But the closer we are in strength, the harder it is for me to hold back. Admit defeat. Even this replica could have killed you instantly if I'd hit you in the wrong place."

"I've always been a sore loser. I thought you knew that."

"Push yourself any more, and you *will* lose." All emotion vanished from Sairi's face. "I was never going to separate you all forever. But this is premature. We need to be patient until the country gets on track. I thought you understood that, Ouka."

"Why should Shiren and I have to live apart?! We're sisters!" shouted Ouka, glaring hard at Sairi's blank face.

This was the first time Ouka had ever verbally acknowledged Shiren as her sister.

"I mean, sure, there are probably plenty of justifications! But if you think I'm going to let adults pull us apart based on any of those, you are gravely mistaken! If my baby sister wants to come home, then I'm going to fight to make sure she can!"

Shiren unconsciously balled her hands into fists.

"Big Sis…"

Ouka was clearly fighting for her sake.

"Aren't you glad Shiren isn't coming back to the Empire, though…?" Sairi glanced at Ryouta.

Ouka drew her lips into a thin line.

"…"

"See? Our interests align."

"…Ha-ha-ha! I see your true colors now, Sairi Fuyukura!" Ouka gave a hearty laugh, as if dispelling all her ill will. "You were never doing this for Shiren. You were doing this for yourself. What do you mean, 'our interests align'? You're hopeless. Your daughter is much more of an adult than you are."

"I—I wasn't… That wasn't… Look, I need to protect the new Empire…"

Sairi went pale. The truth she had been trying to hide even from herself had slipped out, just like that.

"You aren't wrong, though. If Shiren comes back, I'll only have more rivals. I won't deny that. But…" Ouka was brimming with the pride of a ruler. "Even though she's naive and childish, my baby sister still managed to use all her strength and smarts to create an opportunity to tell us she wants to come home. I have to take her back—I don't have a choice. If I can't even make my only sister happy, how am I supposed to do it for a whole nation?"

At some point during this conversation, Ouka's wounds had begun to close. That must be due to her awakening; she could heal much faster in this state.

"You're small, Sairi Fuyukura. You're like a little puppy that's all bark and no bite."

Sairi readjusted her grip on her sword. "Say what you like. I'm going to win."

Even Ryouta could sense the obvious bloodlust emanating from her.

This wasn't good—Sairi wasn't going to go easy on her this time.

"Ryouta, help me out here."

Shiren grabbed Ryouta's arm. She didn't wait for an answer, but she didn't have to. There was only one answer he could give.

"Okay. Be careful."

Shiren bit into Ryouta's arm…

…and sucked his blood.

It was tentative. Nostalgic. She was careful at first, but as she got used to it, she drank more. The flavor was a reminder of simpler times, and it made her heart beat harder and faster.

"Oh, Ryouta. I finally figured out why I never felt fulfilled here."

"What?"

"No matter what kind of delicious foods I ate, I could never find a replacement for your blood."

"You must not have been eating very well if you couldn't forget that."

"The best dish in the world couldn't replace your blood. It's not about flavor—your blood is precious to me."

Jet-black wings sprouted from Shiren's back, ripping apart her dress.

Unlike Ouka, Shiren didn't have enough Sarano blood in her. Half of her was not Sacred Blooded—it was human. And so her wings were not formed from light but took physical shape, like bat wings.

But that didn't mean she was powerless.

"I'm here to help, Big Sis." Shiren, wings spread, stood beside Ouka. "No, wait, that's not exactly right. I should be forging my own future with my *own* hands. I shouldn't have let you fight on my behalf."

"You've matured since you moved, Shiren. Why don't you stay a little longer and continue your studies?"

"I got bored of it. I want to go back to the old Empire for a while."

"How cheeky of you."

The two sisters smiled at each other for the first time in a long while.

"Shiren... Move. I can't hold back now... I have to concentrate on putting my all into this fight."

"Don't hold back, then. I'm going to put my all into this fight, too—for my own future."

Clearly, she wasn't going to pull back anymore just because her mother asked her to.

"Then I'll make sure she can't concentrate." Ryouta had moved to stand behind Sairi.

Ryouta wasn't strong enough to join in this fight. That said, no matter how powerful Sairi was, she couldn't attack on two fronts at the same time.

She could cut down Ryouta easily, sure, but that would require her to turn her back to Ouka and Shiren.

"You're going to die, you know... No one with their head screwed on right would try and interfere."

"But I'm Ouka's minion and Shiren's friend. If I didn't try to help, I wouldn't be human."

"Fine. Then first, I'll make sure you can't move."

Sairi whirled around and rushed at Ryouta, but she seemed a little different from before. She was panicking. She'd forgotten about biding her time. If they could make her panic just a little more, then they could win. They just needed to wait. That said, if Ryouta fought her head-on, he'd die.

I don't plan on doing that anyway. After all, this wasn't a one-on-one battle.

Ryouta reached out toward the tablecloth to his side and pulled with all his might.

A giant white sheet appeared in front of Sairi. For a second, she flinched. She didn't know exactly where Ryouta was. But since she was already in motion, she didn't stop.

The moment she stepped into the tablecloth's embrace...

...the other two rushed at her from behind.

"This is *child's play*!" Sairi yelled. She sliced the cloth in half, but Ryouta was gone.

"You missed!" Ryouta brandished his sword.

She could easily block his attack, but then she would be unable to stop the two behind her.

As she whirled around, two hands reached out toward her own, gripping her sword. She was a seasoned fighter—she could have thrust Ryouta aside and then fought back against the other two.

But when she saw her daughter, she balked for just a moment. As she sliced through the air, her sword went off course, and the girls' hands grabbed on to Sairi's.

The hands wouldn't cut into her, but the force was more than enough to eject the weapon from her hands.

Clatter.

The sword fell to the ground. The fight was over.

Despite how powerful she was, Sairi could not take down two awakened Sacred Blooded with her bare hands alone.

The room went quiet. Shiren stared at Sairi. Her mother's eyes were still brimming with bloodlust. But there was no sound. No words.

Slowly, Sairi raised both her hands.

"You win." At last, the tension eased, and a grimace crossed Sairi's face. "What can I do when the emperor herself commits treason? It seems the new order of the Virginal Father is having a rough time of it, too."

"You're nowhere near strong enough to carry the Virginal Father's standard!"

Kiyomizu was just finishing up with the new order. In the battle between new and old, victory had landed in the hands of the old.

"Fine. I'll carry on by myself, like I've always done."

"Mom…"

Shiren knew Sairi's loneliness well. It was a lot like her own.

"I don't need sympathy. I'm too selfish for that. I'm a bad adult, and I lost. That's all."

As the battle came to a close, they heard the *ding* of an elevator arriving on their floor.

"Oh dear, what bad timing. I wonder if someone called the police."

Sairi didn't know who it was, but she was sure they'd be shocked at the scene before them when the elevator doors opened.

"Oh! You must be Sairi."

A girl wearing a big ribbon on her head stepped out from the elevator. Perhaps not a *girl*—she was short, but she seemed much too calm to be a child.

"Who are you?"

"*Ehem*, I have come to deliver a message to you. *Ehem, ehem...* I worked so hard, my cough is acting up again... It's so dusty in here..."

"Rei? Where were you?!" Ryouta was shocked at Rei's unexpected appearance. He'd never expected to run into her in Japan.

"Oh, Ryou, you're here! This must be destiny. But I'm sorry—I need to deliver this message before we have our touching reunion hug. I don't want to forget again and have to go through the trouble of going back to the other side."

"Who is this message from?" Sairi was bewildered, unable to follow the conversation.

"Someone named Owen... Oh, no, sorry—Ouen."

"What?!" Sairi's voice cracked. "That cannot be. He is dead... It must be an impostor..."

"A long time ago, you went to an eating contest in Tokyo, but you'd gone to a buffet just before and had to forfeit partway through. If you'd gone in without eating beforehand, you definitely would have won."

"Wh-why do you know about that...?"

It seemed Rei was telling the truth. Sairi's mouth hung open in shock.

"You were so disappointed, you went to a Korean barbecue place to eat away your stress, and that's when you met Ouen."

"Huh, that's not a very romantic story..." Ryouta couldn't help but speak up. "And why would you go for Korean barbecue if you'd just lost an eating contest...?"

"A few hours passed, and I got hungry again."

Despite coming from the former competitor herself, the answer wasn't very convincing.

"That's when Ouen turned to you and said, 'Are you eating alone? So am I. Let's eat alone together.'"

"He did. I then ate a surprising amount, and through tears, he declared he would pay half the bill. He said making me pay for what I ate would hurt his pride as a man, but he didn't have enough to pay for both of us."

"There's not a shred of romance in that story…"

"But you've only just met me. How do you know all that…? Were you another one of his girls on the side…?" Sairi looked at Rei dubiously. Ouen was apparently a notorious cheater.

"No! I would never do something so immoral! I only have eyes for my little brother, Ryou!"

Her statement was problematic for a different reason, but pointing that out would only cause trouble, so even Ryouta let it slide.

"And even if he was cheating with me, he wouldn't tell me a story like that!"

"I guess you're right… So how did you learn this, then…?"

"I'm often on the brink of death, and it was during one such time that I met him on the other side, *ehem*. He tried to seduce me out of the blue…"

"He was always, always like this…" There was anger and exasperation on Sairi's face. She'd never imagined she'd be hearing about his scandals in the afterlife, too. "Fine. I'll believe that you met him on the other side."

"Very well. Then let me give you this message before I forget—'I'm sorry.'"

Those two words caused Sairi's mouth to fall open. There was a fragility about her; it was hard to believe she'd been in the midst of battle mere moments earlier.

"'I'm sorry, Ominaeshi. Sairi. If things have soured between the two of you, I am to blame. I want you to hate me, curse me to die. Well, I'm already dead, though. I'm a child. I could never love just one person.'"

"Oh, boo-hoo. I'll be sure to hate you and more, just as you asked."

"'And so, please hate me alone. No one else. Don't let this affect the girls.'"

"…"

She had known their words and actions would affect their daughters. There was a small part of her that had acknowledged it was inevitable. But hearing it put so clearly into words gave the statement a power beyond what she'd imagined. It sounded as if she'd pretended not to know, and he was blaming her for that.

"'No one can choose the circumstances of their birth, and sometimes, that is painful. But adults who understand the unfairness of life should never take that out on children.'"

"I know, I know… No, actually, maybe I never knew…" Sairi continued to listen, not looking at Shiren or Ouka.

"'Unfortunately, I can't solve your problems for you, but I know you'll be okay. And one last thing—this is a little embarrassing, but I can't send a message and not say it. Sairi, Ominaeshi, Ouka, and Shiren…'"

The daughters made quiet noises in response to hearing their names.

"'…I love you.'"

It was a mundane phrase, but it held special power for Sairi, Ouka, and Shiren.

"'I love you. And that's why I hope you'll stay away from here for some time to come. I'll be fine on my own. Keep on forging through life'… And that's the end of the message."

Sairi collapsed to her knees. Tears were flowing down her face. The control she had been trying so hard to maintain had been shattered in one fell swoop.

At this point, there wasn't much she could do. Even if she tried to calm herself, her heart was going in every direction at once, and she couldn't rein it in.

"I'm sure you have a lot to say, but you may cry for the time being, *ehem*. Everyone, please leave her be."

Perhaps Rei was able to understand Sairi as a fellow adult, because she remained calm even as she watched the other woman cry.

"I don't really understand what's going on, but nice work, Rei."

"Gosh, I really did my best! Could you give me a pat on the head?"

"I guess so."

Ryouta slowly ran his hand over her head. It wasn't easy, though, considering how her big ribbon got in the way.

"Hee-hee-hee~. This was worth dying over and over for~!"

©Hiroki Ozaki

That was a pretty high price to pay for a head pat.

"But this Ouen guy sure is selfish. Look at all the women he's made cry. I'm not very impressed."

It didn't sound like Rei had a very high opinion of Ouen.

"And he reminded me a lot of you, Ryou."

"What…?!"

"Ah, I can see that. He sweet-talks everyone, just like Father."

"I agree with you, Big Sis. I can see it."

For some reason, Ouka and Shiren started staring at Ryouta dubiously.

"I guess the one difference would be that Ryouta's totally unaware of it. Father was always gung ho about seducing women."

"He'd always loiter around high schools and universities, saying he was 'observing.' He *must* have been there only to look at the girls. Just thinking about it is making me angry with Ryouta, too."

"Hold on… Why is your impression of me getting worse just because you think we're similar…?!"

"You really need to do something about that personality of yours, Ryouta; otherwise you'll end up dead, just like him. I think there's a very high probability of it."

"What………?"

"Actually, if you manage to survive as long as our dad did, you should consider yourself lucky."

"I—I really don't get what's going on, but……I'm sorry." Ryouta bowed, still baffled.

Funnily enough, he'd chosen the exactly same words to apologize as Ouen had.

"If *sorry* was enough, you wouldn't need a gravestone."

"If *sorry* was enough, you wouldn't need *manju* at your funeral."

"Wait! Why are you both acting like I'm going to die?"

Ryouta did not like the direction things were moving in.

"No need to worry. I'll be sure to live a fulfilling life even after you're gone."

"Don't kill me off yet!"

"When you die, I vow to take responsibility and eat all the leftover funeral *manju.*"

"That's a stupid thing to make a vow over!"

The sisters were relentless.

"Shiren, I think you and I have more in common than I originally thought."

"I was just thinking that."

They giggled, and their laughter sounded oddly loud on the quiet battlefield.

Shiren's

Heroine Danger Rating!

Ouka   Danger: ★★★★★
I'm a little scared since I know it'll all be over if she decides to use her rights as emperor.

Sasara   Danger: ★★★★★
Big Sis is gently keeping her at bay, but I think things would go south pretty fast if she wasn't.

Alfoncina   Danger: ★★☆☆☆
She's surprisingly introverted and shouldn't be a problem.

Tamaki   Danger: ☆☆☆☆☆
I mean, it's Tamaki...

EPILOGUE

"Ahh, this flavor really does make me feel at home."

Shiren was drinking some miso soup in the Fuyukura home, which was neither very big nor very new. Ryouta had arrived in the morning to make it for her.

Ryouta continued to live in his seemingly haunted apartment in the castle. He couldn't possibly sleep over at the Fuyukura house, where Shiren was living alone.

Incidentally, Shiren was still in her pajamas, which already made everything seem very informal.

"I even made the broth out of dried sardines. Though I know it's nothing compared with the stuff they had at the hotel buffet."

"Look, restaurant food is restaurant food. You're not supposed to eat it every day. Your simple miso soup is way better."

"Really? Thanks. Hearing you say that makes coming here to cook it all worth—"

"I think I'll customize it by adding tomatoes."

She plopped a whole bunch of tomatoes into her soup.

"I'm actually starting to wonder if I should trust your sense of taste…"

It didn't seem as though her eating habits had changed very much, even after having such fancy food every day.

"Ahh~. The simple life really is best. I don't think I'm suited for serious work like that of an emperor."

"I'll have to agree with you there."

As she lazed about the room, Shiren flipped on the TV. There was nothing special airing. But in a way, Ryouta was thankful for that.

On the screen, some text read, *The Great Emperor's Little Sister, Lady Shiren—Her True Life.*

"Hey! What on Earth?! I didn't hear anything about this!" Shiren grabbed the TV and yelled at it. Of course, no one at the TV station was going to hear her.

"Calm down! You'll break the TV!"

But as it turned out, the program was talking about how Shiren had left Oshiro to work on creating peace among all the Sacred Blooded—painting her in a very favorable light.

"Hey, so they do understand! The world is finally acknowledging my greatness and beauty."

"They've really edited this to make you look good. But I guess they don't want to harm the image of the emperor's little sister. And by the way, they haven't talked about your beauty at all."

"Next, we discuss Lady Shiren's academics. It is said her grades are very low, and her performance is disappointing."

But things then took a turn for the worse.

"She has reportedly gotten zero points on her world-history test. This cannot be good considering she leads a country, but we must trust that gives her a flexible point of view and novel thoughts not bound by common logic."

"Hey! Don't exaggerate my grades, you terrible reporters! I got two points! Not zero! I got one question right!"

"That's barely any different! It's basically the same!"

"But it's *not* the same! Wouldn't you rather get two snacks from your friend when they come back from a trip instead of zero?!"

"That has nothing to do with grades!"

"I could score a hundred points by getting two points on fifty tests. I'd be stuck at zero forever if I got nothing but zeroes."

"Yeah, I guess that's *technically* right, but that's not how tests even work!"

"Oh, it looks like we've been lazing around so long that it's almost time to go."

VIPs from other countries were visiting that day.

"I guess you've got your hands full, being the emperor's little sister and all."

"I can't change that."

"Who's coming today? Do you know?"

"Not sure, but probably dignitaries from Japan. Big Sis wants to start getting more involved in international diplomacy."

And with that, Shiren went to change out of her pajamas and into her formal clothes.

"You're late, Shiren. You're two minutes behind schedule."

When they arrived at the castle, Ouka was wearing a dress.

"But if I'm late, where is everyone else...?"

"I asked you to come fifteen minutes earlier than everyone else."

"Why do you always treat me like I'm chronically late?!"

"Oh, there's no specific reason. Maybe it's just my way of gently harassing you?"

"I don't care if it's gentle! Stop it!"

Ryouta watched the exchange with a little sigh.

But it's true—things are a lot more fun this way.

A relationship where everyone said what was on their mind was much better than one built on superficial niceties.

Though I feel like openly saying she's harassing her is a bit much...

"But you're right on time, in a way. One of our guests has already arrived."

Ouka's gaze settled on someone behind Shiren.

"It's been a while...or has it?"

It was Sairi.

"Mom..."

Shiren hadn't thought she'd be seeing her mom so soon.

"I invited her as an official guest today. We can't keep fighting forever."

"I'm glad to see you, Shiren. Things have finally settled down in the New Sacred Blood Republic, too."

When the Holy Sacred Blood Empire's emperor left, Sairi became president and made the country a republic, replacing *holy* with *new*. There had been a bit of a shift in their principles, but there hadn't been too much chaos. Japan, too, had ostensibly approved the change.

The same was true of the old Empire. It had been declared that the

©Hiroki Ozaki

new country would be recognized because they'd acknowledged a single emperor. As such, reconciliation was progressing on both sides, and this fact had already been reported in the news.

"Though I'm so busy as president that I don't have a lot of time to get away."

Sairi wasn't brimming with rage as she had been before; right now, she was positively maternal.

"I'm sorry for causing you so much trouble..."

Shiren, however, still felt a little guilty. Sairi had single-handedly managed the chaos Shiren caused when she left, after all.

"It's fine. This is my job as your mom. And I'll be by to say hello every once in a while."

"Okay!" Shiren replied enthusiastically. She was, of course, happy to see her mother more often.

"There's one more person I need to see today."

"She should be coming soon, so just hold tight. I asked her to arrive an hour earlier than everyone else."

Ouka apparently trusted this person even less than Shiren.

"Goodness... I haven't walked this much for a very long time..."

In staggered Ominaeshi, carrying a cane with a skull on it.

"I know your legs and hips aren't so weak that you require a cane. Can't you just walk like a normal person?" Ouka was fed up with her mother.

"Coming up to the surface drains me of so much of my strength..."

"The surface? We're still inside..."

"Oh, you're already here."

The moment Ominaeshi saw Sairi, she tossed away her cane and straightened up. It appeared she really didn't need it.

"To tell you the truth, Sairi, it was I who asked that you be summoned here."

"You?"

"Mm-hmm." Ominaeshi bashfully extended a hand. "Let us be friends from now on... Shall we? For the sake of our daughters' generation. What fools we must be to quarrel over that dirty cheater, Ouen..."

Sairi snorted and took her hand. "Then let's hate him, just like he asked in his message."

"He said it himself, so I see no problem with it."

Ryouta watched their exchange, feeling that the parents' generation had finally reconciled. But not a moment later, a hint of spite crossed Ominaeshi's face.

"I will be the one to win our next *Smash Br*s* match, however…"

"I can beat you with one hand tied behind my back." An easy, confident smile crossed Sairi's face. She was clearly belittling her opponent.

"What cheek… I grow stronger by the day, you know…"

"Unfortunately, you'll have to get a *lot* stronger to beat me. I've crushed you in *M*rio Kart* and *P*yo Puyo* and *B*mberman M*motaro Railway*."

"You're gamer friends?!"

It sounded like they'd played more than a few times together.

"Then come to the basement, and I will show you a true challenge!"

"I'll take you down in an instant."

They started making their way toward the lower floors. Were they seriously going down there to play games?

"Oh, I forgot." Sairi whirled around before leaving. "Ryouta?"

"Yes?"

"Take care of Shiren for me."

There was a smile on Sairi's face. But to Ryouta, this wasn't something he could answer lightly. His face tensed as he said, "All right."

"Good. I'm holding you to that."

With that, the two mothers headed underground.

"Oh, right~. Ryouta? This is totally off topic, but…" Ouka beckoned Ryouta over with one hand. In the other, she held a piece of paper.

"Hmm? What is it?"

"…you still owe me two hundred thousand yen for this month's rent. Any update on that?"

The paper read:

BILL
200,000 yen is owed for the rent of castle room 1313.
Sacred Blood Bank Account Number: xxxxxx

*   *   *

"You're taking money from me?! I thought it was free!"

"Of course it's not free. You still pay the company for company housing, don't you? Hurry up and pay me."

"Uh, I'm pretty sure company dorm rooms like that are usually really cheap…"

"We have a saying here in the Sacred Blood Empire: *This is us, that is them.*"

"I'm pretty sure that's an old trick grandparents use to shut kids up!"

"Because your room is haunted, I even lowered the regular rent of two hundred ten thousand to two hundred thousand. Pay up."

"That discount is practically nothing!"

There was no way he could afford it. Even an adult would have trouble paying two hundred thousand yen a month for an apartment.

"You're always there, too, though. Can't you let it slide…?"

"Legally, it's still your room, so no. Wait a minute, you'd ask your girlfriend to pay for use of your room when she visits? Unbelievable."

By that way of thinking, charging your guards that much rent was also unbelievable.

Not like I can argue with the emperor, though…

"Haah, I guess you won't be able to live there." Ouka gave a heavy sigh. "And I suppose I have to do what I have to do as your landlord."

"You're my *landlord*?!"

"School is *so* far…"

"This is good exercise! Think of it as part of a healthy lifestyle, and it'll make things easier. Deal with it."

Shiren swung her arms with delight.

"I don't really think I need to improve my lifesty— Ow."

There was a tug on his arm. Ryouta and Shiren were holding hands as they walked.

"Hey, aren't you, like, embarrassed about this?"

"We're friends. Why would I be?" Shiren's answer came easily, and Ryouta decided not to argue.

"Good morning, you two."

Tamaki stood at the school gate, wearing the library-committee armband.

"Morning, Tamaki!"

"Morning, Shijou. I feel like it's been a long time since I last saw you wearing that armband."

"Yes. I (literally) let loose all the things that had been building up inside me, and now it feels as though everything's been reset. I feel thoroughly refreshed and decided to put it on again. I still feel no love for books, though."

"I see you're still not really a fit for the library committee."

"And to make matters worse, I ordered a hundred thousand jam rolls and a hundred thousand copies of *Kairakuten* again, so I have to come up with a whole new way to get rid of them... I should really have rewritten the purchasing agreement..."

"I don't think you're a good fit to work at a convenience store, either, Shijou..."

Tamaki chuckled. "If it doesn't suit me, then I'll just have to search for a new job."

"Wow, that was surprisingly optimistic of you."

"Yes. I've started thinking differently. If I am to die one day, then I might as well try everything. We all return to oblivion upon death, so what does it matter if I cause a few problems...?"

It sounded like her core personality was still the same, however.

"Actually, Her Excellency the Archbishop scouted me, and we'll be forming an idol group called *Unhappy*."

"What kinda weird things is she up to now...?"

And that was a horrible name for an idol group.

"Apparently, our concept is to have each of our fans buy ten or more CDs so I can pay back my debt."

"Your concept is way too real!"

"Good morning~! Tamaki, we'll be starting dance lessons next week!"

Just then, Alfoncina cut into their conversation.

"Alfoncina, can you not get all these people wrapped up in your shenanigans?"

"Hee-hee. Hearing that from you, Ryouta, considering all your shenanigans, is rather convincing."

There was no need for her to be rude, but there was truth to what she'd said.

"I'm not getting involved in any more shenanigans... I get the feeling I'll be in real danger if I keep that up..."

"I think it's a bit too late for that~. I'll be sure to pray for you, of course! Mmkay?"

Alfoncina suddenly pulled Ryouta into a hug.

"Hey! This is too much!"

"It's just a little hug! We've had each other's blood, remember? We're already very close."

"No, we haven't! You only drank *mine*... Can you just get off me, please?!"

"Yeah, Alfoncina! Let him go!" Shiren grabbed Alfoncina to pull her away.

"Ryouta is my........."

Her momentum petered out.

".........friend."

As a friend, she couldn't claim exclusive possession of him. And how close could they get as friends anyway?

"Hee-hee~. Things turned out like this because of Ryouta's decision. It's not my fault." Alfoncina laughed, keeping a tight hold on him. Her breasts were pressed up against him, likely deliberately.

He decided not to think about the soft, squishy sensation. Even though Shiren didn't seem all that mad right now, he knew she was going to explode sooner or later.

"Please just let go of me. I'm going to be late."

"You're right. See you later, then, Ryouta, my minion!" Alfoncina said with glee as she dashed off.

If things keep up like this, it's going to get worse when I reach the classroom.

Ryouta was beginning to remember how tiring his daily life had been. And there was still another obstacle between him and the classroom.

"Good morning, Ryouta dearest!" Kiyomizu was waiting for him.

I'm never going to get to class at this rate...

But Kiyomizu seemed a little calmer than usual.

"Did you know, my dear, sweet Ryouta, that your curse should be vanishing soon?"

"What? Are you talking about the curse that makes human women attracted to me...?"

His grandfather, who had led a long, sad life of being repulsive and unattractive, had prayed that his grandson would be the exact opposite—and that grandson was Ryouta. Despite his grandfather's good intentions, Ryouta had found his life in danger a good number of times and had come to consider the whole thing a real hassle.

"I'd be really happy if it went away. But why do you think it will?"

"When I was back in Japan, I did a little research on the prayer. And I actually found one that fit."

Of course the Jouryuujis would have that kind of information.

"And the curse apparently weakens when the subject lives life away from the ones it affects. That means, since you've lived among the Sacred Blooded for so long, you are most certainly reverting back to a normal person."

Now that she mentioned it, Kiyomizu *was* acting a little less overboard.

"Are you no longer being affected, Kiyomizu?"

She had been with him since he'd lived in Japan, and she had definitely felt its influence.

"No, the effects have faded. I feel that I can stand before you and maintain a rational train of thought, Ryouta dearest."

This is fantastic, thought Ryouta. He had always felt bad for her. He'd felt like he was scamming her by forcing her to like him through the power of the curse.

"Even if you stop being affected, I'd still like to stay friends."

"Unfortunately, I'm here to tell you that's not possible." She immediately refused his request.

I guess it's not surprising she'd wind up hating me…

He'd understand if she hated him for the rest of her life for playing with her adolescent feelings. Ryouta would have been furious if their positions had been reversed. He felt a little sad to think she would be leaving him, but he knew that was selfish.

"I won't ask you to forgive me, but let me just say—Kiyomizu, I'm so—"

"Even if the curse goes away, I'll love you always and forever, Ryouta dearest! And I! Will always! Love youuu! Let's stay together forever!" She leaped onto him and clung there. "Just being friends isn't enough for me! I want to be more than friends!"

"Right. Okay…"

Ryouta sighed—he had mixed feelings about this. Half of him sort of expected this to happen, and the other half was somewhat relieved that Kiyomizu hadn't changed.

"But since the curse is unrelated, that means my feelings are real. Or are you unconvinced?"

"No, I get it, I just… Hold on…"

He couldn't just let her have her way.

"Hold on? For how long? One minute? Three minutes?"

Those were abnormally short wait times.

"At least a day…"

"Ryouta, we're going to class! Get off him, Kiyomizu, you're in the way!"

"I'm not listening to you. You owe me at least a year, so I'm not listening-. ♪"

Kiyomizu was clearly looking down on Shiren.

"That's not true! At most…three days!"

"What?! All that for three days?! That's not fair compensation! It can't be legal!"

"I'm giving my thanks, so shut up. I'll be sure to send you a year's supply of tomato juice as your end-of-year present."

"I don't want that!"

"You two seem a lot closer than I thought," Ryouta murmured, suddenly the third wheel in this conversation.

"Not at all." "Not at all."

Their voices overlapped like they'd been practicing. Way too obvious.

"We're going, Ryouta. Or we'll be here forever."

Shiren pulled on his arm, dissatisfied.

"Uh, okay…"

But the next event was already waiting on the staircase landing. It wasn't specifically waiting for Ryouta this time, but he did happen upon a conversation.

"All right… You said it yourself—you like him. So I'll back off…"

"I'm glad you understand. I really do appreciate how you fought at the hotel, though. But…that wasn't enough to change how I feel."

"Your thanks are more than enough for me…"

It sounded as though Sasara and Toraha were chatting. They were right up against the wall like they were trying to be secretive, but they probably should have moved somewhere with less people.

"Morning. Why are you two chatting over there?"

"Gaaaaah!" "Aaaaaah!"

They yelled in unison. Their reaction was enough to make Ryouta feel like the bad guy, even though he'd just asked them a question.

"R-Ryouta Fuyukura…" Toraha was bewildered.

"Y-yeah? What is it?" Ryouta thought he must be making the same expression.

They'd fought each other seriously before and still couldn't seem to strike up a casual conversation.

Toraha placed his hand on Ryouta's shoulder. "M-make my cousin happy!"

"What? Hold on. I don't understa—"

"You both have my blessing… But in exchange…I won't forgive you if you ever make her cry… Farewell! I am off to wipe the sweat I feel gathering around my eyes!" With that, he dashed down the stairs in tears.

Oh yeah, he doesn't go to this school… Did he get called out here first thing in the morning…? But he was asking me to make his cousin happy, so that means…

He had to have been talking about Sasara…

"Oh, you can ignore everything he just said… I have no idea what he was talking about. Ah-ha-ha-ha…"

Sasara was apparently planning on pretending nothing had happened. However, her face was bright red, and she was clearly flustered.

"Goodness, I have no idea why he came all the way out here… What a mystery. So strange. Ah-ha-ha-ha… I am completely in the dark."

It's really obvious she's covering something up, but maybe I shouldn't poke my nose into her business…

Ryouta instinctively chose to ignore her behavior.

"……So you're not going to ask what happened." Sasara stared at Ryouta, her gaze oddly cynical.

"……Well, you said nothing happened."

"Indeed, and I would never lie."

She apparently didn't like how Ryouta was handling the situation, and there were thorns in her words.

"Oh, that's right. An old-fashioned snack store opened up in the class next to ours."

"Uh, why would that happen…?"

But sure enough, there was a sign over the door that read THE FOX'S SNACKS, indicating a store.

Ryouta peeked inside to find rows and rows of typical products—several brand-name snacks, marshmallows, absurdly thin slices of *katsu*, and strange little yogurt pots that came with wooden spoons.

Apparently, Kokoko was running it.

"I figured as much from the shop name, but…what are you doing here?"

"Is it not obvious? I am running my store. *Crunch, crunch.*"

Kokoko bit into a crunchy butter-flavored potato snack.

"I can earn some pocket money *and* snack on food when I'm hungry, so I'm killing two birds with one stone here. *Munch, munch.*"

"So this means you have the school's permiss—"

"I do."

"They really let everything slide here, don't they…?"

"Though when your sister came in wearing a uniform and pretending to be a student, security obviously had to kick her out."

"No, Rei! That's so embarrassing! But I guess even a lax school like this one wouldn't put up with that…"

"And when she tried to run away, she had an episode and collapsed, falling headfirst down the stairs. Then while she was on the ground, several students running through the halls trampled over her, so now she's sleeping in the infirmary."

"Well, I'm sure she'll be up again soon."

Ryouta had no warmth for his relatives.

"Okay, I'm going to cla—"

"Wait, Ryouta. I'm buying three hundred yen worth of snacks."

Shiren was scouring the assortment of snacks rather seriously.

"Shiren? You know the three-hundred-yen rule is for field trips only, right? And you know today's a regular school day and not a field-trip day, right?"

"You mustn't let yourself be bound by tradition," said Shiren, cutting him down with questionable logic.

"If we make the corn-potage flavor our baseline, then maybe natto is a good addition. You could replace the teriyaki-burger flavor one with any snack that has a rich sauce. Or we could change direction and go with crunchy plum. But the crunchy-ramen types are kind of fun. Oh, but the chocolate cigarettes make me feel fancy, so that might be a good choice, too. Hmm. What a hard decision!"

"You should try to put at least half that much effort into your studies."

Shiren bought her snacks, and they finally reached the classr—

"You're late, *minion*." Ouka was waiting for them beside the door.

"Hey, why are you hiding there like an assassin?! You scared me!"

"I was waiting here with one idea in mind: Kill before I can be killed. My minion was terribly late, you see," Ouka said, her tone suggestive.

"Uh... Well, a lot happened, so..."

"A lot, hmm? Don't tell me something happened between you and Shiren at home?"

It was Ouka's turn to look at them with an uneasy expression. She had become a lot more expressive lately.

"Obviously not!"

"Y-yeah, Big Sis! Stop being weird..." Shiren joined Ryouta, denying the accusation.

"I see. That's good." Relieved, Ouka's expression calmed again. "Can you imagine the scandal if you were to *do* something with the emperor's minion?"

"Uh, Big Sis? Um…"

"What? Say what it is you want to say. You'll end up regretting it again otherwise."

"Thank you…for letting me live with Ryouta…"

Shiren was embarrassed about giving an honest thank-you, even to her big sister. No—perhaps *because* it was her big sister.

"Ryouta left the castle because he didn't have the money to pay rent. That's all. I think your thanks are misplaced."

Of course, everyone knew it wasn't a coincidence.

Not everything had gone back to the way things were before. The fact that Ryouta was Ouka's minion still hadn't changed. But Ryouta's life with Shiren was back to normal.

"Well… I'll just say that this way of doing things increases our group's general happiness the most. Even if we're not constantly fighting, sometimes it's a good idea to try and remove the fences between us. I still haven't given up, and I am not giving in." There was true happiness in Ouka's smile. "To be honest, I could easily win if I used my power. But I realized I have no reason to panic. I will do as an emperor must and fight you head-on. And I will achieve such overwhelming victory that there will be no regrets. The fact of the matter is, I am still winning."

Ouka's expression was like that of one who wished to unleash chaos upon the world. Though it was hard to tell if chaos itself was the goal, or if she was merely confident that she would get what she wanted even if she had to take the long way around.

"Of course, this leaves plenty of chances for others to butt in. I'm perfectly aware of that."

Ouka turned to look at Sasara, Tamaki, Kiyomizu, and even Alfoncina, who was watching from afar.

"I have no intention of losing." She slipped her arm around Ryouta's in a natural manner. "Keep serving me well, Ryouta, my minion."

"Uh, okay… But can you not do this in class…?"

The stares he was getting from his classmates were pretty bad.

"It's fine. It's perfectly normal for a minion to stay by their master's side."

"H-hey, you can't keep him to yourself!" Shiren grabbed Ryouta's other arm.

He really did look like a ladies' man.

"You have no right to do that, Shiren. I'm the one who made Ryouta my official minion!"

Ouka gave Shiren an incendiary smile. It was as though she was saying, *Give me your best shot.*

The look Shiren shot back read, *I'm not going to lose to you, either.*

She had to come up with something to say back.

"And Ryouta's my..............friend!"

"Should you be clinging to a friend like that?" Ouka asked, cautiously confirming.

She was speaking to Shiren, of course. Ryouta was also saying something, but they both completely ignored him.

"Y-yes! This is normal for friends, okay?!"

She had to say that, or she'd risk losing. So she gave her answer boldly, knowing perfectly well it was a bit of a stretch.

"......Very well. You reap what you sow, Shiren."

"What?"

Shiren had essentially created a loophole.

"That applies to me, too!" Alfoncina exclaimed.

"Though I may not deserve it, I would count myself as his friend, too...," added Tamaki.

"He's my *boyfriend*, so I can do even more!" Kiyomizu shouted.

"I will not deny that he and I are friends...," Sasara stated.

"I feel like the population density has gotten really intense around me..."

Ryouta tried to protest, but it seemed as though no one was interested in answering him.

"I suppose this is like a game of patience now. We shall see who gives up first," Ouka said.

"I'm not going to lose to you, Big Sis!"

With arms around him from all sides, a thought occurred to Ryouta.

Maybe my curse has just transferred from humans to Sacred Blooded...

"Come closer to me, Ryouta." His master gave him an odd command.

"Wh-why...?"

"Because you are serving me as my minion. And you call *that* service?"

"Okay..."

Ryouta edged closer to Ouka. She was already clinging to him, so it wasn't like he was going very far.

In response, he thought he felt the hold Shiren had around his arm grow tighter.

"I-I'm not losing to you, Big Sis..."

If this keeps up, I might actually die...

He was genuinely frightened for his life.

I need to watch out... I need to watch out for girls...

AFTERWORD

Hello everyone, this is Kisetsu Morita! The *Service* series has at last reached its final volume. The only reason I managed to get this far is because of all your support!

This is the final volume, so I'll be concentrating on my thank-yous. First, to the editors and the sales team—the only reason we managed to reach Volume 7 is because I had your help in selling Volume 1. I've learned so much, what with drama CDs and two manga adaptations. Thank you so much!

To my illustrator, Hiroki Ozaki, thank you so much for sticking with the series for so long. It would have never gotten off the ground if you hadn't drawn Shiren and Ryouta and all the others.

And I owe a great debt to the manga artists, urute and Toshiko Machida. It was so fresh and exciting to put my characters in other people's hands and allow them to come to life. In fact, it almost felt like a feedback loop, where I looked at the manga and saw the way I portray my characters in the novel change. That was especially true for Kiyomizu and Tamaki—I had to be careful, otherwise it'd be hard to tell which version was the original.

Also, this might sound strange, but I'd like to thank all the characters who did whatever they liked throughout the series, all the way up until the end.

Of course, I, Morita, the author, am writing this story, but the longer the series went on, the more I found the characters would do things on their own. There were more than a handful of times where I thought, *Hey, I never planned for you to say that line!* I had to adjust the plot whenever that happened, but it made the story much more interesting when the characters moved on their own.

Kiyomizu, especially, was only supposed to be a stupid little girl character in the beginning, but at some point, she became an old soul and Shiren's big sister figure. At first, Sasara was meant to be a minor character whose only role was to cling to Ouka, but she eventually started asserting herself and often ended up in the spotlight. I was like, "Hey, is this okay?" But I decided to let this series be driven along by its characters.

This volume marks the end of the series, but—and I know this is a cliché line—Ryouta, Shiren, and Ouka's strange lives will keep on going. I decided to end it on a note that leaves the story open for a continuation.

I want to leave the conclusion of the story to all of you who have read this seventh volume. I hope you come up with something good. This may be the end, but thank you so much, all of you, for sticking with me through seven volumes. Thank you, thank you! It was a lot of fun!

Kisetsu Morita